FORGET-ME-NOT

What Reviewers Say About Kris Bryant's Work

Whirlwind Romance

"Ms. Bryant's descriptions were written with such passion and colourful detail that you could feel the tension and the excitement along with the characters…"—*Inked Rainbow Reviews*

Taste

"[*Taste*] is an excellent traditional romance, well written, well conceived and well put together. Kris Bryant has given us a lovely warm-hearted story about two real human beings with whom we can genuinely engage. There is no melodrama, no overblown angst, just two women with an instant attraction who have to decide first, how to deal with it and second, how much it's worth."—*Lesbian Reading Room*

"*Taste* is a student/teacher romance set in a culinary school. If the premise makes you wonder whether this book will make you want to eat something tasty, the answer is: yes."—*The Lesbian Review*

Jolt

"[*Jolt*] is a magnificent love story. Two women hurt by their previous lovers and each in their own way trying to make sense out of life and times. When they meet at a gay and lesbian friendly summer camp, they both feel as if lightening has struck. This is so beautifully involving, I have already reread it twice. Amazing!"—*Rainbow Book Reviews*

Visit us at www.boldstrokesbooks.com

By the Author

Jolt

Whirlwind Romance

Just Say Yes: The Proposal

Taste

Forget-Me-Not

FORGET-ME-NOT

by
Kris Bryant

2017

THIS TRADE PAPERBACK ORIGINAL IS PUBLISHED BY
BOLD STROKES BOOKS, INC.
P.O. BOX 249
VALLEY FALLS, NY 12185

FIRST EDITION: APRIL 2017

CREDITS
EDITOR: ASHLEY TILLMAN
PRODUCTION DESIGN: SUSAN RAMUNDO
COVER DESIGN BY SHERI (GRAPHICARTIST2020@HOTMAIL.COM)
COVER CONCEPT AND COMPOSITION BY DEB B.

Acknowledgments

This book was a journey for me. It started with a trip to Ireland and ended with love.

I will always be grateful to Bold Strokes Books for continuing to publish my style of writing and my type of romances. Thank you, Sandy and Radclyffe, for trusting my voice and supporting me and all of us. We are all so different, yet a part of a wonderful blended family.

Without Ashley, my books would never solidify into something enjoyable or complete. She does a fantastic job of keeping me on task and isn't afraid to tell me strengths and weaknesses with everything I write. She's my rock and I really couldn't do this without her.

Thank you, Deb, for always looking out for me and giving me the space to write these romances. I know it's not easy, I'm not easy, and this process takes a lot out of me. And Molly. She's right beside me during every step of the way. I love you both.

Every year I meet new writers who inspire me somehow, someway whether they realize it or not. I love my writer family. We are a beautiful group who want to share the stories we create. Thank you to the readers who support us and continue to appreciate what we do. Our community is small, but fierce. I am thankful to be a part of all of us.

Dedication

To D

CHAPTER ONE

I have my laptop and several e-books to keep me busy on the flight that never ends, but I'm too nervous to settle down. I'm on my way to Ireland from Dallas via Philadelphia and even though it's only been five hours, I feel like I've been thirty-seven thousand feet in the air for at least a week. Forget about telling me to sleep on an airplane. I never do. I'm the one who suddenly jerks awake and then tries to play it off like I didn't just scare the crap out of myself and my heart isn't somersaulting in my chest. It's just better if I stay awake.

The little old lady in the seat next to me is knitting and humming. She hasn't said anything to me. She only smiles when we do make eye contact and that makes her my ideal travel companion. Had Morgan, my best friend who was supposed to be on this trip been sitting next to me, I wouldn't get a word in edgewise, nor would I have this much peace. The book I'm reading isn't holding my interest, so I decide to pull up photos on my laptop of places I want to see while I'm in and around Dublin. That gets the attention of my neighbor. She stops knitting and stares at the screen.

"Oh, that's a lovely town there," she says. I smile at her Irish accent and obvious delight in what she is seeing on the screen.

"My great aunt lived there for many years," I say.

"Are you visiting her?" she asks. Her eyes light up and I'm surprised at the melancholy that has suddenly weighed down my heart.

"No, she recently passed away. I'm going to sell her flower shop and see to her affairs," I say. She gives me a pat on my arm and I give her a sad smile.

"I'm sorry to hear that." She is quiet until she sees a picture of Ireland's Eye, a small island just off of Howth. "Oh, that's a fine place to see. Lots of history there." She proceeds to tell me a little bit about the tiny island accessible only by boat.

"Do you live in Howth?" I ask.

"Oh, no. I have a cottage in Dalkey, just outside of Dublin. My husband and I used to go to Howth on the weekends. Such a quaint, lovely fishing town. We always wanted to get a place there, but it is very expensive." I wonder how hard it is going to be to sell the shop if the cost of living there is astronomically high. Is anybody going to want a flower shop? I probably should have done more research on the town and the shop before I jumped on a plane.

"Is somebody picking you up when we land in Dublin?" I want to change the subject because I'm starting to panic as the weight of the burden of selling a business in a country that isn't booming economically starts settling in.

"My grandson, Sean, is picking me up. He's such a good young man. He's about your age, I think," she says, squinting her eyes at me, either sizing me up, or trying to figure out how old I am. She tells me her name is Ailis and she has been in New York City visiting her son who moved there ten years ago. Her daughter still lives in Dublin with her two sons, one of them Sean, who will greet her at the airport.

"That's very sweet. I thought about staying in Dublin overnight, but decided I'm just going to take a cab directly to Howth. I'm supposed to work with a representative from The Mulligan Group tomorrow."

"That company has been around for years. They are very popular around Dublin. You should have no problem selling the shop." She picks her knitting back up, my story no longer interesting to her. I take her cue and put in my earbuds. It isn't long before I hear the pilot over the speaker mumbling something and pull my earbud out just in time to hear him say we are beginning our descent. I want to look out the window, but the sun is getting low and I'm sure Ailis doesn't want me to lean over her. I pack away my laptop and try to calm my nerves as I wait for the wheels to hit the tarmac.

"Not a flyer, eh?" She smiles at me. I look at her and she looks at my hands on the armrests, my knuckles almost white. I release my death grip on the metal arms and calmly rest my hands in my lap. "I don't blame you for being nervous. The flight into Dublin is usually pretty bumpy. It's really not too bad this time." She says this as we are still five thousand miles up in the air.

"I just can't relax. There is something about being this high up without any control." I stop myself from thinking too hard about it because I don't want to say anything or freak out and upset Ailis. She's more upset by the flight attendant asking her to put away her knitting.

"You should have been on airplanes forty and fifty years ago when people smoked and the seats weren't comfortable. Turbulence like this would have given you whiplash," she says. The horrified look on my face makes her laugh. "So just be happy today's airplanes are much more regulated and cozy." I know we are close to hitting the tarmac, so I put my arm out and rest my hand against the chair in front of me, bracing myself. Surprisingly, it is quite smooth and several passengers applaud the pilot's skillful landing. Now I allow the excitement of a new place to envelope me and I look out of both sides of the plane, hoping to see something more than airplane towers and other planes. No such luck. I lean back and anxiously wait for the plane to empty.

"Well, good luck, dear. I hope that your trip is successful and that you fall in love with Ireland." Ailis picks up her bag and smiles at me before she slips into the line of people waiting to get off the plane. I take a moment to gather my things and work my way into the single file line slowly walking to the exit. Thankfully, I only have my carry-on and messenger bags so I head straight for the customs line. Feeling nervous and anxious because this is all new to me, I explain that I'm here on business and perhaps some pleasure if there is time. The stoic official stamps my passport and hands it back to me, my life unimportant to him as he dismisses me and waves to the next person in line. I head for a restroom to freshen up and take a moment to collect myself. When I exit the restroom, I stop to get my bearings and people watch. I'm very surprised at how many people have flowers. Every single person I see has a smile on their face. Morgan is so wrong. People need flowers. I remember I promised to call her when I landed.

"How do you always know to call right when I'm ready to take a bite of food?" Morgan doesn't believe in answering her phone like a normal person.

"Please tell me you are eating a chicken parmesan sandwich from Johnny's. I'm starving," I say. She answers me with a grunt and a lot of lip smacking noises. My stomach rumbles.

"How was the flight?" At least that's what I think she says between mouthfuls of her lunch.

"It was, you know, awful. I made it though. Now I'm going to figure out how to get out of this airport and get to Howth." I know I'll hire a cab, and I'm now considering hiring a driver all week because driving on the other side of the road freaks me out. That was supposed to be Morgan's job. A driver will be quite the expense, but well worth it. Or I can become familiar with public transportation.

"Remember to take a few days for yourself. Go find a hot Irish woman and have fun. Keep it light. Pretend you're me," she says. I'm entirely too shy so I know that's not going to happen.

She's the one who gets all of the action when we go out. I can usually be found hiding in a corner, sipping on a fruity, weak drink. I'm confident with everything in life but women. I snort at Morgan's advice. "Grace Danner. You listen to me. Quit selling yourself short. You are a beautiful woman inside and out, and people want to be near you. Don't let one crappy relationship ruin the possibility of something incredible, even if only for a few days. She was just stupid. It's time to move on." We don't ever say her name. When the big break-up happened, Morgan, my warrior, my heroine, couldn't get what's-her-name's stuff out of my condo fast enough. She showed up with storage tubs and boxes and the ex's stuff was gone within a few hours. To this day, I still don't know what happened to it all. I can only assume that the ex received it because I never heard from her again. Either that, or Morgan had her killed, hid the body, and gave all of her stuff to a homeless shelter. "How about when you get back, we make a serious effort for both of us to find girlfriends."

It's amazing how quickly I stopped caring about finding my soul mate. "Are you ready to settle down?"

"We are both thirty-one years old and not getting any younger. Plus, it would be nice to have somebody to come home to. I haven't really done that," she says.

"It's not all it's cracked up to be."

"Quit feeling sorry for yourself. You were born to be a wife. You just need to weed through the crazies to get to your Princess Charming. And I need to open up and let somebody in. It's time." Morgan has been my best friend since college. She's always felt this need to protect me, and I do what I can to keep her grounded. We are a good match, as friends only.

"I'm not worried. Maybe I just need a break. Sometimes it's best to disconnect in order to reconnect." I roll my eyes because that even sounds cheesy to me.

"Thanks, bumper sticker. Now go and sign papers and eat food. Oh, and be sure to kiss an Irish girl. If not for you, do it for me." I'm smiling when I hang up the phone. Morgan always knows how to get me in a good mood.

❖

I wait in the taxi line and smile at the attendant who asks my destination. His accent is very thick, and at first I don't understand him so he repeats himself, speaking slower this time.

"Howth. The Walsh Bed and Breakfast please," I say. The taxi driver looks immediately annoyed. I'm sure he wanted a fast trip so he could hurry back to the airport and collect his next customer. The attendant loads my bags in the trunk and taps the car to signal to the driver that he is good to go. It takes the driver a good five minutes before he starts talking.

"Are you in Ireland for business or pleasure?" I'd rather he didn't ask boring questions and just let me enjoy seeing what little I can still see of Ireland in the dimming twilight.

"Hopefully a little bit of both," I say. He nods like he understands.

"From America, huh?" This time I nod. "Where in America?"

"Dallas, Texas," I say. That perks his interest.

"Texas. The land of cowboys and jeans," he says. I'm tempted to kick my leg up onto the armrest to show off my Ariat boots, but I refrain. Suddenly, I have a fan. He starts talking nonstop about western movies and how people in Texas have the best of everything. He either has watched too much American television, or not enough.

"It is a great place," I say. He bombards me with a bunch of questions all at once. "No, I don't have a horse, but I do like to ride. Dallas is probably three times bigger than Dublin." He's very excited when I launch into a little bit of history about Dallas. When I finally shut up, he starts in about Dublin's history and before I know it, we are in the small town of Howth.

"Here we are," he says, putting the car in park. He jumps out and opens the door for me, gathering my luggage from the trunk before I'm out of the car. I must have given him a large tip because he thanks me again and again and hands me his business card. "Please call me when you are returning to the airport or need a cab to get around." He slips back into the cab and quickly darts off.

I unlatch the wrought iron gate and get a good look at the old stone house. I wonder how long it's been there and how many coats of paint have peeled off the shutters. It is old, but quaint and I smile at its charm. The beautiful red door opens and I'm greeted by an older lady who fusses over me immediately.

"Come in, please. Before you catch a chill," she says. I'm fairly certain she knows who I am since I'm expected, but I'm still surprised at her friendliness. She offers to help carry my bag, but I insist that I carry it up the steps. She's half my size and about thirty years older. "I'm so glad you made it." The yellow and red floral wallpaper brightens the room somewhat, but doesn't disguise the age of the place.

"Ms. Walsh, right?" I ask politely. I don't want to assume she's the owner, but I want to give her respect in case she is. She nods. "What a delightful place you have here. I was admiring the outside. When was this built?" I hope that's not an insulting question. Apparently not as she begins to teach me about the house and the neighborhood. The house was built in the eighteenth century and doubled in size when the family decided to open the bed and breakfast close to one hundred years ago. The kitchen tripled in size, and a third level was added including three guest rooms and three small baths. Ms. Walsh has put me up on the third floor because the floor is better insulated and the bathrooms are relatively modern.

"I'm sorry the room isn't larger, but the shower is hot and the room has a beautiful view of the Irish Sea," she says. She is a mixture of proud and embarrassed.

"It's perfect," I say and mean it. It's amazing to think about the people who stayed here in this house even before it was a bed and breakfast.

"If you're hungry, I can open up the kitchen and cook you something," she offers. We both can't pretend my stomach didn't just growl.

"Please don't bother, Ms. Walsh. I can just run down the street. I'm almost certain we drove by a restaurant," I say. She's one step away from fretting about my nourishment. "I've been sitting for the last twelve hours. A walk and fresh air really would be nice." That appeases her. She directs me down the street to Sullivan's Pub. I walk that way and can hear it before I see it. As I round the steep corner, I'm greeted by two older men outside smoking pipes. One gallantly opens the door for me.

"Niall, quit flirting. She's here for a pint not an old man like yourself," he says. After a few days, I'm sure I'll get used to the accent here, but for right now, I can't help but smile. They could tell me that there is a murderer out and about preying on American women and I wouldn't even care because I'm under the spell of the thick Irish brogue. I enter the pub and swear I've suddenly teleported two hundred years into the past. This pub is everything I expected it to be, only better. There are long tables and only a few booths for eating. Most of the patrons are sitting at the bar talking, laughing, and drinking. There is no television, no music, just people having several different conversations at once. Feeling self-conscious because I appear to be the only woman in the joint, I freeze. Do I go to the bar? Do I sit down at a table? A booth?

"Take a seat anywhere." A voice booms out at me and I quickly sink into the closest booth, desperately trying not to draw attention to myself. A few patrons look my way and nod, but turn back around to their conversations. A woman in her late forties, early fifties heads my way digging a pencil out of the hair piled haphazardly on her head. "What can I get you to drink?" She's perfect. Exactly what I expected to see. Plumpish with meaty hands and a warm smile. Her hair is more brown than red, but curly with frizzy strands bouncing out from her scalp. The pencil she now holds was keeping most of her hair contained.

"Is it too late for food?" I ask. At this point, I'd nibble on dry bread crusts.

"I can get you a bowl of Irish stew. It'll warm you up quite nicely," she says.

I nod with approval. "And I have to try a Guinness, too, while I am here."

"Where in America are you from?" she asks. I don't even bother asking why she thinks I'm from the United States. From what I understand, Europeans can spot an American from five miles away.

"Texas," I say.

"There it is," she says. I have no idea what she means. "Your accent." I smile. Her accent is far sharper than mine.

"Is that a good thing?" I ask.

"Of course. Wait a minute. Are you Nola Burke's great niece?" she asks, her smile fading quickly. "She was such a nice lady. We are all sorry she passed." I feel guilty that I'm not as affected by her passing as they are, so I only nod my appreciation of her respect.

"I'm here to handle her shop and get things in order," I say. She pats my hand.

"Let me get your food and pint and I can tell you more about your aunt," she says. I watch her walk away and mumble something to the bartender. He nods at her and looks at me. Feeling self-conscious, I look away and study my surroundings instead. This pub is so unlike anything I've seen back home. It is designed for people to share meals, talk, and drink. Nobody has their cell phone out. I hear music from somewhere, probably the kitchen, but it's faint and not a distraction. I find myself relaxing even though I'm in a new place and don't know a single soul. Within five minutes, I have a bowl of hearty Irish stew and soda bread in front of me, accompanied by a glass of beautiful, dark stout.

"You will have to come back for lunch when my boys deliver the fish. Freshest fish and chips you will find here in town," she says. "I'll be back in a moment to check on you." I dig into the stew and sigh happily as the flavors dance inside my mouth. The stew is perfectly seasoned with just the right amount of vegetables and meat. I soak up the broth with the bread and even though the beer is strong, I manage to get through half of it while wolfing down my food.

"Was it to your liking?" she asks, swooping in to gather up my bowl and plate.

"Fantastic. It hit the spot," I say.

"I'm happy you enjoyed it. The stew is an old family recipe. I'm Colleen Sullivan, the owner here," she says, still busying herself around the booth, wiping up imaginary crumbs. I invite her to sit down and she gladly accepts.

"Your aunt was a lovely woman. She kept mostly to herself, but everybody knew her. She came in here quite a bit for lunch. The flower shop she ran is just a few streets over and on nice days, she would walk here for exercise."

"I didn't really know her very well. I think the last time I saw her was the summer after my high school graduation. We had a family reunion when my grandfather retired in Florida and I spent a few hours talking with her. She was always nice and friendly," I say.

"Oh, yes. Very quiet, but very popular. The men around here always asked her advice on love and how to keep the fire going," she says. I look at her peculiarly and she laughs. "When you have a flower shop, you know the best way to a woman's heart. You know what to do." I smile. I forgot about that part. I thought maybe she was Ireland's Dear Abby. I have so much to learn about the power of flowers. "She probably saved more marriages than she realized."

"I know so little about her," I say. "I don't understand why she chose me." She didn't have any children, but plenty of other family members who, I'm sure, were more involved in her life than I was.

"Well, there is a reason she did and I'm sure you will figure that out in due time," she says. "I should get back to work. Don't be a stranger. And come back for lunch." She yells at one of the men who is ribbing her about sitting down on the job. "I will be seeing you, Grace Danner." She walks away before I even realize that I never told her my name.

CHAPTER TWO

I don't sleep the greatest when I travel, so I'm not surprised when I'm up before sunrise. I know that I'll be toast by noon, but right now the excitement of being in a different country and wanting to explore it gets me ready and dressed. I'm supposed to meet Kerry Mulligan at nine thirty at the flower shop. That gives me almost three hours to sightsee and explore the village. Just under nine thousand people live here so I can't imagine that I will get lost or be unable to find the shop.

"Grace, breakfast isn't served until seven," Ms. Walsh tells me, her face registering surprise as she almost bumps into me in the foyer. I'm getting my camera equipment ready and not even thinking of food.

"Oh, I'm fine. I just want to get a head start on this gorgeous day," I say.

She fusses for a bit, tells me to wait, and comes back with a warm pretzel roll with cheese and butter tucked inside. "This should tide you over until I can get a proper breakfast on the table."

"This will tide me over until lunch." I never eat breakfast back home, but if somebody brought me this every morning, I would rethink the three meals a day thing. This smells heavenly.

I head out, anxious to begin my journey. I zip up my leather jacket all the way when I'm greeted by a biting chill in the early morning wind. Thank God I left without putting makeup on because the tears that keep slipping out of the corner of my eyes would have washed it away. I head straight for the docks. Howth is a little fishing town and I'm excited to capture its essence with my camera. The houses that line the street leading down to the water are colorful and laced with age. It's hard to believe that this town has been around for over a thousand years. Dallas is under two hundred years old and already there is a lot of renovation to buildings and parks. I'm pretty sure these houses have been here for at least that long. Charming with age. I take a few photos of the colorful doors that I've read about and head to the docks. Several of the boats are already gone, and the ones left are either unloading their pre-dawn haul or just there for weekend trips. I snap a few photos of the fishermen, surprised that several of them are younger than I am. I hear a wolf whistle coming from a docked boat, but ignore it and focus on the seagulls floating on the air above me. They are everywhere, waiting for the fishermen to throw scraps of fish into piles, scavenging from ten feet above. I take pictures of them, my nearness not affecting them at all. When I spot a pair of sea lions breech the surface, I squeal and get as many photos as I can before they disappear under the water. What a fantastic sight. I crawl down over some rocks to look out across the water. It's so peaceful here. I eat my roll, sharing a large portion of it with the fish and birds. I smile because I know that if Morgan was here, she would still be in bed, mumbling about how cold it is. She would never crawl over these rocks and sit on mossy, cold stones eating a sandwich and feeding fish. She would complain about the smells and want, no demand, to sit in the car or find a restaurant and drink hot coffee.

I check my watch and decide I need to find Aunt Nola's flower shop, The Irish Garden, and meet with the realtor. I want to get there early so I can see the shop and its location. Sad to leave my peaceful place, I wipe the crumbs off of my jeans and vow to return to this sanctuary before I leave. Just looking around, I see so many things that I want to photograph. I've almost filled my memory card and I've only been actively snapping photos for the last two hours. I adjust my settings so that I'm able to squeeze more on the card, thankful that I have several empty ones back at the bed and breakfast. This is so unlike Dallas where everything is new and shiny. Even though it's early, there are already several people out, including two families at the playground, young people headed to the coffee shop, and others headed to the wharf. I read that there is a farmer's market out on the wharf and I plan to hit that before I leave.

I look back at the docks and notice that the early morning sun is hitting the tips of the boats, giving the entire harbor a beautiful warm glow. I snap a few pictures, but I'm not quite at the angle I want to be so I step out into the street to get that perfect shot. That's a mistake. I hear screeching tires and a loud crash beside me. I freeze and tense up, waiting for a giant truck to smash into me and send me a hundred yards down the street. I slowly turn to the side and see a Volkswagen Jetta crunched into a concrete and stone garbage can, the fender and part of the hood crumpled up. Holy shit! I forgot the Irish drive on the opposite side of the road here so I literally walked into traffic because I was looking the other way. Before I even fully cross the street, the driver's side door flings open and a woman busts out yelling at me. She flings her arms at me, then points to the car, then back at me. I can't keep up with what she is saying, so I just stand there and wait for her ranting to stop.

"I'm so sorry. I didn't mean to jump out in front of you." I'm about two feet in front of her and suddenly I forget I just caused her to crash her car. She's gorgeous and every bit Irish. Long, red hair, alabaster skin, and emerald eyes. Morgan has green eyes, but this woman's eyes are a dark green, a color I have never seen before. She's still ranting at me and I still don't understand her. Her brogue is too strong, or she's speaking a dialect, or Gaelic. I pick up on a few words that aren't entirely pleasant, but I don't blame her.

"Why would you jump out in front of my car? Who does that? Why didn't you look first?" Finally, words I understand. She stops talking, her chest rising and falling fast at the adrenaline coursing through her. She moves closer to me, her stunning eyes flashing with anger. She is waiting for me to say something.

"Are you okay? Are you hurt anywhere?" She looks completely and justifiably perturbed. "I'm so sorry," I say again. "I forgot that you drive on the opposite side of the road here. I will pay for all damages to your car." She stares at me, looks back at the car, then back to me. I see her shoulders slump. I feel stupid standing there, looking at her and saying nothing. I have no idea who to call to fix her car. I've been here twelve hours and I've already managed to screw things up. Now I wish Morgan was here. She would take complete control of the situation.

"You're American," she says. There is no malice in her voice. As a matter of fact, she suddenly seems sad at that revelation. I'm thoroughly confused. "Let me guess, you're Grace." Okay, now I'm completely confused. I haven't been here long enough for people to talk about me.

I nod. "I am. How do you know me? Who are you?" Before I get the final word out, I know who she is. She's Kerry Mulligan, the realtor I am to meet with right now. "Let me guess. You're Kerry," I say. She turns from me and heads back to her car. I'm standing on the edge of the street wondering what I'm supposed to do now. She crawls into the car and grabs her cell phone. I head over to the car to investigate the actual damage. The front bumper is curled up and is pushing up against the tire, making it immobile.

"Luke is coming to tow the car," she says.

"I really am sorry. I can't believe I did such a stupid thing," I say. I glance over at her and see her hands clench into fists. If this wasn't such a serious moment, I would smile at how much she is struggling to keep her anger in check.

"I know it was an accident," she says. I think she is trying to convince herself of that, and not me. I'm suddenly very glad she's the agent and works for me, because her fury fully unleashed would probably make me weep. She makes a few quick calls and suggests we walk to The Irish Garden. The three block walk is hell and done in painful silence. I glance at her a few times, admiring her slender form and her feminine grace. Even her cool demeanor is attractive. Once we turn the corner and I see the shop, I'm quite impressed with it. The front is bright and colorful, not gaudy, and the large window boasts flowering plants and vases of cut flowers. I'm surprised to see a cat perched on the windowsill, inside, close to the door. I smile and rub my finger at it on the outside. It rubs up against the window, trying to feel my hand. As I wait for Kerry to unlock the door, I take a moment to look at the shop's location. It seems to be in an easily accessible place. There is ample parking across the street and the shop is visible from the intersection. There is only one neighbor; a small electronic store that is about half the size of the flower shop, but just as quaint. There is a long stone wall covered with ivy and moss on the other side, hiding whatever is behind and beside the shop.

"I normally don't do commercial real estate," she says as she finally gets the door to unlock. She steps back and motions for me to enter in front of her.

"Then why are you doing it now?" The question comes out snottier than I intended and I see her stiffen. I tone it down and ask it a different way. "I mean, why did you take the contract?" She flips on the lights and I take a moment to look around. She answers me when I turn to face her.

"I liked your great aunt. She was very sweet and kind," she says. She offers me no other explanation and instead starts talking about the size of the shop and what's included in the sale. "You have approximately three hundred square meters in the store, ninety square meters for storage, and another sixty for the office. That is also the same amount of space above for your aunt's living quarters," she says, pointing up at the ceiling indicating where my great aunt lived. I look at her in surprise.

A brief whisper of a smile flashes across her face, but it is gone before I have a chance to truly appreciate it.

"I guess I just assumed my great aunt lived elsewhere," I say.

"Most people who have businesses have living quarters in the same place. Ireland isn't a wealthy place," she says, the bitterness back in her voice. I inwardly sigh. Either she was really attached to her car, or she is pissed that I'm here. Knowing my luck, it's probably both. I follow her around the store, impressed by all of the different flowers and plants on display. The cat in the window weaves its way toward us, anxious for a real loving session. "Why hello, Abram, how are you today?" Her voice has changed from professional to charming and the cat rubs up against her legs, relishing her touch. He purrs and meows and ends up falling at her feet, offering his furry belly to her. She squats down and loves on him for a bit. I take the time to walk around the store, touching soft leaves and smelling wildflowers. I've never seen most of the flowers in this shop. It's a nice change because back home, there are about four different flowers that I have ever seen or paid attention to. Roses, carnations, tulips, and lilies make up about ninety-nine percent of the bouquets I've sent or received. Here I can really only identify lilies.

"There are so many great flowers here. I don't know many of them," I say. She walks over to me, Abram snuggled in her arms. "Is he my aunt's cat?" Suddenly I'm hit with the realization that this cat might be an orphan and now I'm responsible for him.

"He's a stray that the shop took in. I'm sure Leigh would take him when the shop sells," she says. She puts Abram back on the floor and points to the office. "The way upstairs is through the office." She marches past me and I fall into step behind her. Now that I'm only a few feet behind her, I can appreciate her form as we climb the steps. Her curves are hidden beneath a suit that is a half size too large for her, but I can still make them out. She is about four inches taller than I am, but about two inches are heels. Because of her slight form, she seems taller. "It might be cold up here. I opened a few of the windows for fresh air." My great aunt's place is surprisingly fashionable. The furniture is so retro, it's actually modern again and in really good shape. The sofa and recliner are a neutral color and contrast well against the dark mahogany coffee and end tables. Most of the personality of the room is punctuated by colorful artwork. Turns out my great aunt was pretty hip. She has an old fashioned radio that I reach out and turn on for no reason other than to keep my hands busy.

"I really like this place," I say. It's about the size of my condo back in Dallas, only not as modern. I don't see a dishwasher or microwave in the kitchen, but I do see a gas stove and I can't help but turn on the burner. "I love cooking with gas."

"How do you cook now?" Kerry seems confused.

"I have an electric stove now and I don't like it so I don't cook very often," I say. "Plus it's hard to just cook for one person."

"You are not married?"

"No. Most of my meals come from the microwave or from the Chinese restaurant on the corner," I say. I can't tell if she's horrified at the fact that I nuke my meals or that I eat Chinese food. Her lips are pursed tightly and her scowl isn't pleasant.

"I always thought that was an exaggeration," she says. So it's the microwave.

"I work quite a bit during the week and get home late so my meals are sketchy," I say.

"What do you do for work?" she asks. She seems genuinely interested.

"I work for an advertising firm," I say.

"For print or television?"

"Both. I mainly dabble in print and layout, but I head their media department, too," I say. Finally, I've impressed her.

"It sounds like you have an important job," she says. I shrug at her, but secretly I'm trying not to smile. "How long will you be here before they can't work without you?"

"I'm here just shy of a week, but if we need longer to seam

things up, I can take more time. Thankfully, I can work out of the office. Most of what I do is approve campaigns or give suggestions to our teams." I don't tell her that we have six teams that keep me busy or that I do a lot of the photography for ads because I have a hard time trusting our photographers to capture exactly what I want. Hence, my sixty to seventy hour work weeks and zero love life.

"Sounds interesting. I'm almost certain we will be able to wrap this up in a week."

"One question, I noticed when I was looking at places to stay a lot of houses and apartments come fully furnished. Do you think I should do that with Aunt Nola's stuff?" I correct myself because I sound heartless. "I mean, offer her furniture and belongings since it seems to be a popular thing to do here. Or, if anybody who works here at the shop wants anything of hers, I'm more than willing to give it to them."

"I think you should do whatever you want to do," she says. She is not helping me.

"What do you normally do? As a real estate agent or as somebody who probably knows what to do in a situation like this." Getting information out of her is not easy. "A little bit of help here would be great." Now she's starting to get under my skin and not in a good way.

"It's really up to the seller," she says. I grit my teeth and just shake my head. We stare at each other for a few moments. She senses my frustration and gives in first. "In your situation, unless you want to box up and ship the furniture somewhere, we can list it as a furnished apartment included with the sale."

"Thank you." Jesus, how hard was that? "This might take me longer than a few days. Maybe I'll tack on a week so I can get through all of her things."

"We aren't done with the property. I need to show you the best part." The tension in her voice is replaced by appreciation.

"Oh?" I lift my eyebrow at her. She does that almost smile

thing at me again and asks me to follow her. We head through the kitchen to a door almost hidden by a closet.

"Be careful and watch your step." She points down to an uneven first step. Again I follow her up. When she opens the door, she turns to me and gives me a smile that makes me weak in the knees. I'm not expecting that. I grab hold of the railing and give her a quick smile back. We walk out onto the roof and I understand why her smile is so large. This is fantastic. The roof was a getaway for my great aunt. There are plants and flowers everywhere. A cute wicker patio set faces the Irish Sea. I'm instantly mesmerized. It's a beautiful view. There is even a hammock off to one side and as tempted as I am to jump in it, I refrain. I walk around, soaking in the beauty and peace of this slice of paradise.

"Wow. This is incredible, Kerry. Absolutely gorgeous." She's still smiling at me and I have a strong urge to keep that beautiful smile on her face. "I hope my aunt spent a lot of time up here. I know that I would if I lived here."

"I think that with this bonus, you won't have any problem selling the property," she says. She is all business again. I honestly can't keep up with her mood swings. She quickly looks at her watch. "I bet Leigh and Emma are downstairs now. Would you like to meet them?" I nod and follow her back down the two flights of stairs until we are back in the office. A woman is sitting at a desk reviewing paperwork. "Leigh, come meet Nola's great niece, Grace Danner. I will be working with her in handling the property," she says. A thin, wisp of a woman stands up to greet me. She is in her late fifties, early sixties with salt and pepper hair and a pleasant face. Truthfully, she could be from any of the last seven decades, her practical, cotton floral dress timeless. Leigh reaches out to my outstretched hand and cups it in both of hers.

"Oh, dear. I am sorry about Nola. She was quite the lady." She holds my hand a little longer than necessary and stares at me. Suddenly self-conscious, I carefully remove my hand.

"It's nice to meet you. This is a beautiful shop. You've done a wonderful job with its upkeep," I say. I can be charming. Even Kerry smiles at me. Weak knees again.

"Has she shown you around then?"

"Yes, Kerry has been extremely kind in showing me the property." I confess that I accidentally made her crash her car and the look on Leigh's face makes me feel ten times worse.

"Are you all right?" At this point, I really just want to slip away and start this day over. Leigh must sense my discomfort because she does an about face and is charming once again to me. "Well, obviously Kerry is fine and Luke will take care of things." We all turn and look when we hear a bell announcing someone has entered the shop. "Oh, look. It's Emma. Good morning. Please come over and meet Grace from America." A very pregnant and beautiful young woman walks over to us, careful not to trip over Abram who wants her attention, and stretches out her hand to greet me.

"Grace. It's nice to meet you. I'm just sorry it's under these circumstances." She tucks a few strands of hair up into her bun, the color as pretty as Kerry's, and I wonder how long hers is. "We really admired your aunt. She was a very nice lady."

"I wish that I knew her better. She's been over here so long that I have only visited with her a few times back in the States," I say. I don't tell them it was only twice because I already feel the two strikes against me. One, I caused Kerry to crash her car and two, by selling the place, I am going to put three employees out of their jobs. I'm not about to lose any more respect they might have for me because I've made no effort to get to know Aunt Nola. My heart is even heavier now that I know Emma is pregnant and she will be out of a job soon.

For the next fifteen minutes, I politely listen to Leigh explain how the business is run and how there are ups and downs depending on the season, the social events, and the age of people in the town, but I'm really trying to overhear Kerry and Emma's conversation. They seem very friendly with one another and I wonder if they are about the same age. Maybe they went to school together or attend the same church. There are so many little churches in this town, I don't know which ones are historical sites and which ones are active. When Kerry reaches out and puts her hand on Emma's tummy to feel the baby kick, I know they have serious history. "So what are your plans while you are here in town? My husband and I would love to have you over for dinner one night if you aren't too busy," Leigh says.

"That would be wonderful. Thank you very much for your hospitality. I know this is a big change for you." I don't know how to apologize to somebody who is about to lose their job. Even though it's not my fault, I know it's my responsibility and I feel horrible.

"We will treat you to a home cooked Irish meal," she says. Damn, if it's as good as the Irish stew I had last night, I'm going to want to stay and eat my way through Ireland.

"That sounds lovely. Any night is fine. I will spend several nights here at the shop going through Aunt Nola's belongings," I say. I know I will have to go through every piece of paper up there and ensure it goes to the right person or place. As much as I want to get to know Howth and the neighborhood, I'm going to have to stay focused so that I stay on schedule. Hopefully they won't mind if I head upstairs after a few more minutes of pleasantries. The door boldly opens and we are interrupted by a thin young man with a mop of dirty blond hair who apologizes for scaring us.

"Ladies, good morning. Sorry for being late," he says. He runs his hand through his hair, pushing the long curls from his forehead. He is tall, pale and borderline unkempt, but charmingly so. I instantly like him. "I'm Conor. You must be Grace." He is not shy and briefly I think he might be flirting with me, but I see he is this way with all of the women. He leans past me and places a quick kiss on Leigh's cheek. He focuses his attention back on me and I'm stunned by his copper colored eyes. "It's nice to meet you. When did you arrive?"

"Last night. I'm ready for a nap. Jet lag and all," I say.

"I've never flown before but I understand it can be challenging," he says. He turns his attention back to the rest of the women. "What's in store for us today? Any new deliveries?" Leigh motions for him to follow her to the back to review the orders of the day and I'm left with Kerry and Emma. Feeling very awkward because now I'm the third wheel, I gingerly step away under the guise of looking for Abram. I'm sure Kerry can't wait to tell Emma about our initial meeting. I inwardly cringe again recalling the scene from just an hour ago. We hear the bell again and I see a large man wearing navy blue coveralls enter the shop. He's all muscle and looks like he's been playing rugby since birth. A true bulldog of a man. I'm actually frightened.

"Where are you, missy?" Knowing my luck, he's looking for me.

"Which one of us are you looking for?" Emma asks. I struggle a bit to understand her when she slips into her dialect.

"Come here, you." He gently scoops up Emma into a bear hug until she squeals.

"Da, be careful. You don't want to hurt your back again," she says. He reaches out and grabs Kerry, too, although with her he is a bit gentler.

"Don't worry about me." He hands Kerry a set of keys. "Here. Take my car. Sean is loading up yours right now. It's not as bad as you think. We just need to pop out the hood, bang out the bumper, nothing major. I'll have it back to you by the end of the week." I quietly slink over to them, my presence forgotten.

"I'm so sorry. Please let me know how much the repairs are going to be and I'll pay for them. And whatever the cost for the car she will be driving until hers gets fixed." He turns to me and I almost take a step back from his size and intensity.

"So, you're the one who jumped out into traffic?" He barks out a laugh. "Oh, boy. I wish I could have seen it. Kerry's temper is always a pleasure to see." He's rewarded with a small punch in the arm from Kerry.

"Luke, be nice. My temper isn't that bad," she says. A pink flush splashes across her cheeks and neck.

"She is very understanding," I say. He nods his head at me sarcastically, knowing full well she had a burst of very colorful and explicit language before reining in her rage. "I know I would have been very upset, but she really did not take it out on me. Please just let me know the costs. I'll still be here by the end of the week. And even if it doesn't get fixed by then, I'll give you my credit card number."

He softens his look. "I'm sorry to hear about your aunt. She has always been nice to my girls here and to everybody in town." He turns back to Kerry. "Now, give me your keys so we can get out of here and let you girls do what you need to do. I'm leaving you the Focus." He waves at everybody again and leaves as quickly as he came. Emma doesn't act surprised so I know Kerry must have told her.

"What do we do now? Do I need to sign papers or go to your work?" I ask. Kerry waves me off.

"Oh, don't worry. I'll get the paperwork together and run it back out Monday or Tuesday. Does your mobile or handy work here in Ireland?" I stare at her blankly.

"Your cell phone. Can you receive international calls and such on your phone?" Emma is quick to translate what Kerry is asking.

"Oh, yes. I had my carrier add international to my cell before I made the trip." Good call, Morgan. I silently praise her decision for insisting I upgrade my plan. I give Kerry my phone number. "Oh, and give this number to Luke, too, please. I don't know how car insurance works over here, but since it's my fault, I don't want you to have to pay a deductible or anything."

"We will figure it out, Grace." That's the first time she's called me by my name. It sounds musical and I find myself staring at her lips. The soft Irish lilt mixed with her raspy voice gives me a quick chill and I look away in case she starts getting uncomfortable. Kerry must be the kind of woman who gets a lot of attention and is completely clueless about it.

"Okay. Well, I will leave you ladies and head upstairs to get started." I give them a half wave on my way to the back of the store. I scold myself for attempting to be friendly. I'm not their favorite person right now and we aren't friends.

CHAPTER THREE

With the windows closed, the temperature upstairs is comfortable although I'm eyeing the fireplace. I can't even remember the last time I sat in front of a fire. Not that I have time to relax, but I can only imagine it being very comforting. The only fire I see in Texas is when I'm grilling. I will have to ask Leigh if the fireplace works. Daydream over, I decide Aunt Nola's desk is the best place to start. Judging by the look of her place, she is extremely organized so I say a quick prayer that she managed to keep great records. I open up the main desk drawer to find a large brown envelope addressed to me along with other documents, paper clipped in alphabetical order. I definitely did not inherit her organizational skills. I'm careful when I open the envelope. A wave of melancholy washes over me as my fingers brush over old photos carefully banded together with blue ribbon. I immediately recognize a few faces including my parents when they were first together, and my grandfather fishing with his brothers. The rest of the papers forgotten, I thumb through the stack of photos, a roller coaster of emotions as I realize most of the people in these photos are long gone. Thankfully, Aunt Nola has written on the back of the photos so I know who, what, when, and where they were taken. Her handwriting is smooth and calming. I find a color photo of her and another woman smiling and seemingly celebrating. I turn the photo over for more information, but find that she only has the name Kate written on it. I guess the photo to be about thirty years old based on how young my aunt looks and the style of clothing she and the mysterious Kate are wearing. They are smoking fat cigars and laughing. I pull the photo out from the rest of the stack and slip it into my back pocket. I want to know more about this photo and about Kate. I see a photo of the flower shop and my aunt standing proudly outside the front door. I flip it over and see that it's from twelve years ago. Everything looks the same. I have a feeling change doesn't come to this community very often. I keep that photo, too, and box up the rest. I'm surprised to find out that going through just the photos has taken up over an hour of my time. I get up and stretch for a moment, and am startled when I hear a scratching noise at the front door. I hesitantly crack it open and am greeted by Abram who mews his way past me and heads for the windowsill. He curls up as if he's been doing this his whole life. I leave the front door open a crack so he can leave again when he's done napping and head downstairs for a quick break. Now that Kerry is gone, I feel like I can be myself around Leigh and Emma.

"Are you done already?" Leigh asks.

"Oh, no. I'm just taking a quick break. Thankfully, Aunt Nola was very organized and I don't think this should take me long," I say. Leigh nods, turning her attention back to a bouquet she is working on. Yeah, that probably isn't what she wants to hear right now. "I just went through a stack of photos. It was fun to see photos from her past. Do you happen to know how long Aunt Nola lived here in Ireland?"

"I think for about twenty years, if not longer."

"I found a photo of her standing in front of the flower shop. It's a great shot. I'm surprised she didn't have it hanging up by the register. Does the shop bring in a lot of business?"

"People here are very loyal to local businesses. We try hard to support one another when we can," she says. "What do you think of this arrangement?" I study it for a bit.

"I think it needs a complementary color, maybe a blue flower if you have it. There are a lot of earth tones and I think a bright color might tie it all together nicely."

"You have a good eye, Grace. Just like your aunt." She heads to the back and returns with a few sprigs of a wildflower I haven't seen before.

"What kind of flower is that?" I ask.

"It's a wildflower that's very popular here. A forget-me-not," she says. I watch as she cleans the stem, plucks the green leaves, and keeps only the small, yet bright blue flowers. She adds them to the arrangement and I smile at the transition of the bouquet. What was a nice, albeit boring display, is now vivid and cheerful.

"It's beautiful, Leigh. Amazing that one tiny flower can make such a difference," I say.

"Oh, this flower might be small, but its meaning is big," she says. "It's hard to get these flowers into bouquets because of their size, but we don't mind using the entire stalk. It's nice to have flowers along the stems and not just the tops."

"I think I might have seen these flowers used as a ground cover more than for bouquets. Back home in Texas, we have blue bonnets and some blue bells." I'm surprised that the arrangements here are a bit more rustic. Several arrangements have wildflowers and they remind me of when my mom and I used to pick flowers in the fields behind the house where I grew up. They are gorgeous, just different from the deliveries I've either sent or received.

"There are several varieties of the forget-me-not. This one works the best for when we need a bit of color. Plus it's a good flower for any occasion. Love, death, and everything in-between," she says.

"Well, you've done beautiful work and I'm sure whomever is receiving this will appreciate what you've done with it." I decide my break is over and excuse myself. As nice and friendly as Leigh is, I don't want to get attached to her. I head up the stairs back to my aunt's apartment, ready to hit the hard stuff. I find a copy of the deed to the building, her life insurance policy, and her bank statements. I'm still shocked that she left everything to me. According to the paperwork my lawyer handed me back in Dallas, everything is free and clear. I know my aunt didn't have any children, but why me? Why did she pick me out of everybody in the family? She has over thirty thousand euros in her personal savings account. I don't even know what's in the business account. She has a small sedan that must be in the back or in a garage somewhere close that is now mine. Doesn't matter because no way in hell am I driving here, not after causing Kerry to crash.

"Grace?" I hear a gentle knock on the door and find Leigh in the doorway. "Emma and I are headed to Sullivan's for lunch and thought we would ask if you would like to join us."

"I'd love another break," I say. I stand and brush cat hair and dust off of my jeans. "Let me just freshen up. I can meet you downstairs in a few minutes." She nods and disappears. I head for the bathroom, enamored by the claw foot tub and old marble floor, dinged with age, but still full of character. There isn't much I can do except splash some water on my face and wash my hands. I'm tired and I know that if I don't take a nap after lunch, I won't make it to dinner. Traveling overseas is grueling. I feel like I've aged ten years in less than twenty-four hours. I meet the girls downstairs and am surprised when they lock up and shut down the shop for lunch. I can't imagine any store back home completely shutting down for an hour. I find that I actually like the idea. When the girls start walking in the direction of Sullivan's instead of driving, I stop. They stop, too, wondering what's wrong. To me, Emma looks like she is going to birth that baby any minute now and I can't imagine that the two block trek is any fun for her.

"Are you sure it's okay to walk in your condition?" I ask. She laughs at me.

"I walk from the train station to work every day. This baby is not coming for at least another two weeks," she says. I look at her and know that baby is going to be a hefty one. She's all baby. There is little additional weight in her face and arms. Emma is one of the few women I've seen pregnant who actually glows. I can tell she's happily pregnant and I figure that's a safe topic.

"Do you know if it's going to be a girl or a boy?"

"Oh, no. My family doesn't believe in finding out until the baby is born," she says. "Even though I would really like to know, my husband thinks it's bad luck." I can't imagine anyone back home waiting. I don't think I could either.

"Do you have the nursery set up yet?"

"Keagan's been working on it since he found out we're having a baby. We have all the furniture and have it decorated in yellows and greens. I think he's hoping for a boy, but won't come out and say it," she says. "I want a little girl. Do you have any children, Grace?"

"No. I don't even have any pets. It's just me."

"You're not married?" Leigh asks. She looks surprised.

"I'm married to my job, if that counts," I say. Nobody laughs. I'm learning that while work is important in Ireland, it's not their top priority. Family and time spent together is first and foremost. I feel guilty because I only see my dad once a month and he lives in the same town.

"What do you do for work?" Emma asks. I explain my position and even though they seem impressed, they are more surprised when I tell them the hours I put in weekly. "So there is nobody there who could do your job when you are gone? Do you ever get breaks? Are you working from here?"

"I guess I'm a control freak and need to know what's happening in all of the departments I manage." It even sounds bad to me coming out of my mouth. Once we hit the door to Sullivan's, our conversation turns immediately to the delicious smells coming from the bar.

"I was here last night and the owner told me to come back for lunch because the fish and chips are the freshest in town," I say. Leigh laughs.

"So you met Colleen," she says. "She's not afraid to boast and rightfully so." Leigh and Emma take a seat at one of the long tables instead of a booth. I sit across from them and wait for any waitress to arrive. Emma and Leigh don't seem to be worried and continue talking about Colleen and her pub and the history of it. It's the oldest pub in Howth, having been passed down generation after generation. After about five minutes without service, I start getting antsy and perturbed. The table is filling up and a man who I assume is a fisherman, sits down next to me and politely nods hello.

"What's the matter? Are you looking for the restroom?" Leigh asks. Before I am able to answer, a server shows up with three plates of fresh fish and chips and places them in front of us. "What are you drinking today?" he asks. The girls both order hot tea and I order a cola.

"Wow. How did he know what we wanted?" I ask.

"We are sitting at the lunch table. This tells them that we all want the fish and chips special. Besides, there aren't very many options for lunch," Leigh explains. I can't complain. It makes sense. I dig into my meal and stifle a moan at the deliciousness and freshness of the fish. It's perfect. Even the chips are great. Nobody is asking for ketchup or any other condiment to drown their food in, so I forgo my usual staples and am pleased with just the flavors of the food.

"This is delicious," I say. Emma smiles at me.

"One day this food will catch up to me, but right now I'm using the excuse that I'm eating for two," she says. She is eating faster than the fisherman sitting next to me and I laugh at their kind exchange. I notice that Emma is more casual with the locals and her accent stronger. Even though I should understand what they are saying since we both speak English, the dialect is strong and

I have to concentrate and process it differently than the English I hear back home. I'm a few seconds late laughing with them, but I find that I'm still having a good time. I spend the rest of the hour slowly opening up to these delightful women. They are so very different than Morgan and my other friends. Morgan's always worried about matching her shoes with her new blouse, and these women worry about if their town will see enough tourism this spring and summer to keep several of the businesses open. Howth is a heartfelt town and maybe it's like this in small towns back home, but I find this selfless attitude refreshing.

"Are all Irish towns and cities like this?"

"What do you mean?"

"How do you keep it quaint and keep big business out of here? Where I live, there are restaurant chains everywhere. Not to mention grocery stores and malls with the same stores over and over. How does this town stay preserved?"

"Well, Dublin and a lot of the larger towns have famous named businesses that you have in your country like Microsoft and Google. And even though Howth is small, we do have takeaway restaurants and pizza places." I smile at their description of fast food. "And it's just a thirty minute ride by train so we really aren't that far out from what you are probably used to in such a big city." I'm positive they would have a difficult time processing downtown Dallas with twenty plus lanes of traffic and every single person in a giant SUV. I have a hard time understanding it myself. My excess suddenly feels gluttonous and I feel guilty for what I've worked for.

"I live in Dublin and take the train everywhere. My husband has the car in case something comes up. I don't mind. The train is a quick, inexpensive way to get to work. If I leave my house at nine in the morning, I'm here before ten. My husband owns a pub in Dublin near Trinity College. As much as I would love to move to a smaller town like Howth, I know that he enjoys the more modern things so a move is out of the question for now," Emma says. "You know, Grace, you should take some time tomorrow and get on the train to Dublin and check it out for a bit." That sounds like a good idea. Tomorrow is Sunday and it's normally my day to relax. I don't think I will hear back from Kerry until Monday so I decide to at least take half a day to explore Dublin or some of the small towns on the way to Dublin.

"I should and I will since I'll only be here until Wednesday. That doesn't give me a lot of time to finish going through Aunt Nola's belongings and visit Ireland. I'll make the effort though. I've come this far, right?" I tell them about my original trip planned with Morgan and how her list of things to do was probably longer than what we could have handled.

"That doesn't give you a lot of time to get things done here. Are you sure you can't tack on a few more days and stay until next weekend?" Leigh asks. I mull the idea over heavily before answering.

"You might be right. I hope Kerry can rush things on her end so that at least the paperwork is finished even if it takes time to sell the shop," I say and cringe at my lack of sensitivity. Leigh pats my arm.

"We know it's not your fault so please don't feel bad for us. Although Nola's passing was somewhat sudden, we knew it was a possibility. It's too bad we can't afford to buy it from you. The good news is that it's in an ideal location and should sell quickly. Just in time for Emma to give birth and time for Conor to get work with his father this summer on the wharf," Leigh says.

"What about you? What do you think you will do next?" I ask. She shrugs at me like it's not a big deal.

"Don't worry about me. I'm sure something will turn up for me," she says. "Come. Let's give our space to other people and head back," she says. I'm surprised at how many people have crammed into the restaurant. Colleen was right. Nothing could beat that delicious lunch.

I wake up on my aunt's couch with Abram tucked in the corner of my arm. He seems content. I'm wary. I don't have any pets and truthfully, cats scare me. He starts purring when he realizes I'm awake. I pet him for a bit and enjoy the peacefulness and quietness of the moment. I have no idea what time it is, but it's starting to get dark out. I carefully lift him up and put him on the other end of the couch. Papers are in stacks on the floor around me. I have a pile I need to send my lawyer, a pile I need to purge, and photographs I plan to keep. I've managed to clutter my aunt's tidy living room, but at least I've gone through all of the papers I found in the living room and kitchen. I will tackle the bedrooms and bathroom later. Now I need food and to figure out what to do with Abram. He seems perfectly happy up in the apartment, but I don't know if he has a litter box up here or food and water dishes. I head downstairs hoping that Leigh is still around, but the lights are off and the door is locked. Thankfully, Kerry left me a spare set of keys so at least I can get out. I see a note taped to the office door and am relieved that Leigh has given me instruction on what to do with Abram. She did not want to wake me after finding me on the couch asleep. Abram has a pet door upstairs leading out to the rooftop garden so he will be fine. I find his kibble in the office and bring him up a bowl. She tells me two scoops will tide him over until Monday, but I feel guilty so I fill his bowl all the way up to the rim. After checking the doors and windows again to ensure they are locked, I slip out the front door and head to the bed and breakfast. I believe I still have time to eat dinner with Ms. Walsh and any other guests who are staying there. The wind has died down, but the cooling air quickens my step. The bed and breakfast is four blocks away and by the time I reach the front door, I'm ready for anything warm to drink or at least wrap my hands around. The doorknob stings my fingers as I turn it.

"I was wondering if you would make it tonight." Ms. Walsh motions me into the small dining area barely giving me time to take off my jacket. "Unusually cold this evening. Come, let's get you warm."

"Hopefully I'm not too late," I say. Thankfully, she seats me next to the fireplace and I smile with relief as the heat thaws my chilled body.

"We are having potato pancakes, bacon, and eggs for dinner," she says. My stomach growls after hearing the menu and I scoot around in my chair to disguise the embarrassing noise. A plate of deliciousness is in front of me in record time. I find that I cannot stop shoveling food into my mouth. I clean my plate and Ms. Walsh offers me seconds. I decline knowing there is dessert. She brings me a piece of honey and spice cake, and a hot cup of tea. I love this woman right now. I clean my dessert plate and take my second cup of tea upstairs. Even though it's early, I can't keep my eyes open and fall asleep on the bed, fully clothed, contentment settling over me like a warm blanket on this cool night.

❖

Ms. Walsh gives me a DART schedule, a bus schedule, and a cartoony map of Dublin with highlighted points of interest. It's rudimentary and perfect for a nervous tourist. Dublin is just too big to handle in one afternoon so I decide to keep it simple and visit the small villages on the DART route. My travel mate, Ailis, from my flight over is from Dalkey so I start there. She spoke of it so lovingly. I'm not disappointed at all. I jump off, snap a ton of photos of the locals, the harbor, the town itself, and jump back on the train. I do that the entire way up to Dublin and reward myself with street vendor food once I hit the big city. Several of the streets are blocked off and every street corner has a musician or artist drumming up business. It's fantastic. I look around and realize it's not even a special occasion. It must always be like this on the weekends. I take photos of all of the people; some who know I'm taking their picture and some who do not. It's a gorgeous evening and even though I want to stay until deep into the night, I'm not very comfortable yet with the DART so I reluctantly hop back on and head back to Howth. This afternoon was a perfect diversion that kept me away from the heaviness of dealing with Aunt Nola's estate and effectively keeping my mind off the mystery of Kerry Mulligan.

CHAPTER FOUR

Dublin during the week is different than the Dublin I fell in love with over the weekend. It's eleven Monday morning and I'm looking for The Mulligan Group's office. Kerry asked me to meet her there to get started on the paperwork. There are entirely too many people in a tiny space, getting their week started. I stay close to the wall for fear of accidentally stepping out into traffic again. I find the company four blocks from the DART station. It's a spacious place with glass offices and beautiful honey colored wood floors. There is very little privacy so I am able to people watch as I wait in the lobby for Kerry to collect me. I see her in one of the conference rooms, her tall form and vibrant hair hard to miss. I watch her chew on her pen as she concentrates on something in her hand. She is a rare beauty. She is the kind of woman you don't want to disappoint, even if she is wrong. I'm surprised by my confusion about her. One minute she upsets me, the next minute I want to reach out and calm her by running my hand down her arm or stroking her hair. I hate that I romanticize everything.

"Miss Danner?" I turn to face the cute, young receptionist who is hanging up the phone. Hopefully, the dreamy look on my face is misconstrued as sleepiness.

"Yes?"

"They are ready for you now. If you are ready, I will take you to the conference room," she says. I follow her even though I know where I'm going. "Can I get you anything to drink?"

"I would love a bottle of water," I say. I don't know how long this is going to take and I seem to get a dry mouth around Kerry. She nods at me, opens the door to the conference room, and ushers me in. Kerry and I make eye contact. I see her back stiffen ever so slightly. I just don't understand why she is still upset at me. I sigh. My guard is up again. The sooner this is done, the sooner I can get away from her.

"Grace, please have a seat," Kerry says. Her voice is friendly enough, but the smile doesn't meet her eyes. I want to lean back, throw my feet up on the conference room table, and act like the rude American she thinks I am. Instead, I take a seat and stare back at her. She's entirely too pretty to be mad at for long. I give her a taste of her own medicine by leaning back in my chair and crossing my arms. A hint of a smile hangs on her lips, but she quickly brushes it off by clearing her throat.

"Thank you for coming. I thought we would have more space here at the office than at The Irish Garden." I look at the stacks of papers spread out over the table.

"All of these need to be signed?" She nods.

"I've put tabs out on all of the places I need you to sign to make it easier. Of course, please take your time reading through the documents. I will be here to answer any questions you might have."

"Thank you," I say. The receptionist returns with a water and I smile a thank you at her. I don't miss Kerry's scowl and I refrain from shaking my head in disbelief. What the hell did I do to her? I'm tempted to go out and buy her a new car, but somehow she would take that wrong, too. I dig into the documents and try to concentrate on the words. I'm sure Kerry thinks I'm a slow reader, but I simply find it difficult to think around her. I'm very surprised at the amount they are going to list the shop for. I thought maybe it would sell for one hundred thousand dollars, but Kerry has it listed for three hundred thousand euros, which is approximately three hundred and thirty thousand dollars.

"Is the shop really worth this much money?" I ask. When her green eyes meet mine, I actually shiver. She's intense.

"The location is everything. Nola obviously knew what she was doing. The Irish Garden is within walking distance of everything including the wharf, and it's easily accessible from all streets. There is ample car and bike parking. I can't promise that the new owner will keep the store about flowers though," she says. I frown knowing full well that somebody will turn this into another coffee shop or food market. Not a bad thing, but one that makes my heart heavy. I sign all of the pages anxious to be done with this whole exchange. I need to get away from her. I can smell her perfume or lotion from here. It's a sweet, floral scent and makes me smile. I don't want to smile around her. I just want to leave.

"Kerry, can I see you a moment?" An older pleasant looking gentleman opens the conference room door, nodding at me. "Pardon the interruption." She gets up and follows him to an empty cubicle. Their conversation turns heated almost immediately. I can't hear words through the glass, but every few seconds, I see Kerry glance my way. I'm almost positive they are talking about me. I stand up and observe them, no longer caring if they see me or not. I watch as she leans her hip against the desk, her arms crossed defensively across her chest. She nods a few times, then looks at me, but this time she doesn't look away. Neither do I. Eventually, the man she is with turns to see what she is looking at. He breaks our spell and I look away first. Within a few seconds, she heads back to the conference room. I see her heels and shapely legs walk the outside length of the room before the door opens.

"Sorry about that. Do you have any questions so far? Is there anything you need help with?" she asks.

"Who is that?" I ask.

"My father," she says. I want to laugh because I know she just got scolding for something, but we aren't on friendly terms so I let it slide. She sighs and sinks down on one of the conference room chairs. "Look, Grace, I'm sorry for being such a jerk. I know I'm not being fair to you or the situation. Let me review the documents and afterward, I would like to take you to lunch to celebrate."

"You don't look like you want to celebrate. It's okay. I can get my own lunch." I sound pouty even to myself. "I know you're busy."

"I really would like to take you to lunch," she says with conviction. I look away and pretend to review the final pages of the contract, even though I've already signed everything. She's watching me, waiting for my answer. I lean back in my chair again.

"So, are you really this mad at me about your car? I mean, I know you have to be upset about your car, but I gave Luke my credit card and offered to pay for a rental car until yours gets fixed. I love my car, too, but I'm not going to hate somebody because of an accident," I say. That might not be entirely true. My car is incredible. She sighs.

"Let's go to lunch and we can talk," she says. The anger is gone from her face and now she just looks sad.

"Fine." I don't really know if I want to spend the next hour or so with her, but for once she doesn't look like she wants me to die so I guess I can take the chance.

"My brother's pub is just down the street," she says.

I lift my eyebrows in surprise. "That sounds good." I watch as she heads for her office to grab her overcoat. Today is a chillier day than even I expected. I zip up my leather jacket and put on a beautiful wool scarf that I found in my aunt's closet. I wanted to wear a skirt and blouse today, but it's very windy so I opted for jeans again and my favorite sweater when I heard the weather forecast. I try not to focus on her curves as she twirls the overcoat around her shoulders. Her navy suit fits her a lot better than the taupe one from the other day and I find myself appreciating her form. I'm irritated with myself for focusing on her looks so I turn away and concentrate on a corporate newsletter on the table.

"Are you ready?" She ties her hair back with a clip and puts on a scarf. With all of that hair, I'm sure her head doesn't get cold very often. I nod and we head out the front door. Her brother's pub is a short walk away and I slow my step so that I can look around. I'm fascinated by the age of Dublin. The date plaques on the buildings are from the eighteenth and nineteenth centuries.

"How well do you know your own history?" Kerry looks puzzled by the question. "I just find it so fascinating that Dublin is so old. You must have some incredible historical stories about this town, not to mention all of the folklore." She sort of smiles at me.

"Well, the Mulligans have been here for centuries. I could write a book on the shenanigans of my family," she says. "We probably have more black sheep in our family than most." I smile at her.

"I don't know a lot of the history of my family," I say.

"Well, you are Irish, correct?"

"Yes, on my mother's side. Aunt Nola was my maternal grandmother's sister. My father's family is Swedish," I say.

"That's probably where you got your blue eyes from," she says. I'm surprised she knows that even though I'm right next to her. She hasn't made eye contact with me a lot.

"My mom had blonde hair, too," I say. "I've noticed that most of the people I've seen have dark brown hair. Except for you and Colleen. I guess I'm a typical American who thinks all Irish have red hair and green eyes." That gets Kerry to smile. It changes everything about the way she looks.

"You will see more redheads now that we are in the city. We have a lot of different hair colors, but surprisingly not a lot of blondes. Not real blondes, I should say," she says. I'm not about to tell her I highlight my hair. We walk in silence until we get to the pub. I almost walk right by it, but suddenly Kerry taps my forearm and darts inside a door on her left. I only have a second to look up and see that we are at Mulligan's Bar. I walk in and again, I'm surrounded by warmth and charm. What is it about Irish pubs? I watch as Kerry heads to the bar and kisses a jovial, nice-looking man on the cheek.

"Brother, we need a table," she says. "This is Grace from America." I smile at him and for just a split second, I see his smile waiver back at me.

"Grace, it's nice to meet you. Welcome to Mulligan's. I'm Keagan. No tables yet so sit at the bar and have a beer," he says. He shakes my hand and has two people scoot down a couple of seats so that we can sit down. I start to protest, but nobody seems to mind so I shrug off my leather coat and take a seat. Kerry surprises me by taking my coat and hers and hanging them up on hooks near the entrance. Apparently they aren't worried about theft like I am. Keagan's accent is stronger than Kerry's and I have to block out all noise to understand him.

"So, what do you think of the shop?" he asks. I can feel Kerry staring at me, my peripheral picking up on her eyes darting all over my profile and suddenly my mouth is dry. I stumble over my words.

"Um, well, I, I think, I think it's very lovely," I say. "A lot nicer than some of the flower shops back home."

"Dallas, Texas, right?" he asks. So I guess Kerry's been talking about me. Given our start, I'm sure they weren't kind words. I nod. "A true cowgirl," he says. I smile.

"I'm even wearing my boots, but I sure do miss my hat."

He leans over the bar to look down at my boots. I have no choice but to show him. He laughs. "Those are perfect. I love them. Maybe I should get Emma a pair," he says. He puts two

Guinnesses in front of us and disappears for a minute. Realization strikes me.

"Emma is your sister-in-law?" I know my eyes are huge right now as my brain processes the jigsaw of information as it falls into place.

"Yes. She and my brother have been married two years. My brother took over the bar when my uncle passed away. He's struggling to keep this place going," Kerry says. That surprises me judging by the large lunch crowd. "He's so stubborn. I tell him his prices are too cheap, but he says he's helping the college students by offering cheap food and good beer. I need to remind him that he's got a family to consider now. A wife and a child."

"Oh, you're going to be an aunt," I say. She gives me a genuine smile that takes my breath away. I feel a fluttering inside of my chest and have to take a deep breath to keep my confusing emotions in check. "Do you already have any nieces and nephews?" She shakes her head.

"No, this baby will be the first. Emma's due in two weeks, but we are all nervous wrecks," she says. "My da is impossible. He's built, carved, and created so many different things for the baby already. He can't relax. My mother is ready and calm, but inside I know she is as excited as the rest of us."

"I don't have any nieces or nephews either. My brother and his wife have fur babies only," I say. She looks puzzled. "Fur babies. Dogs and cats." She laughs.

"The only animal I even get close to is Abram," she says.

"Who doesn't like pets?" I ask.

"I love animals, but I don't have any pets. How many do you have?"

"I work entirely too many hours to be fair to any animal. Maybe when my life settles down, I'll rescue a dog or a cat. I haven't really thought about cats until I met Abram. He's such a sweet boy," I say. Yesterday, he was upstairs the entire day with me and I enjoyed knowing he was close.

"Agreed. I stay pretty busy, too, but once I save enough money for the farm I want, I will have sheep, goats, dogs, and chickens. Then I won't have to work so much on the real estate side and can make my own hours. And I've said too much," she says, nervously twirling her glass of beer between her hands. It's obvious Kerry doesn't like to talk about herself, especially to me. I take a big gulp of beer for courage and ask what's been on my mind since I got here.

"So tell me why I've been such a sore spot for you. I know I screwed up your car, but I have to think it's more. Whatever conversation you had with your dad just made you even angrier at me and I just want to know why. We're going to be working together and I need some sort of peace. This isn't easy for me."

She sighs. "My stubbornness always gets in my way. I know you're dealing with your aunt's death, but I also know you weren't very close to her. You want to sell the shop as quickly as possible and get back to your life, but I don't think you see the repercussions that selling the place has on us. Jobs aren't as readily available as they are in America. Emma is pregnant and once she gives birth, where is she going to go? She and my brother need the money from her job to survive. And Leigh. She's in her fifties and who is going to hire her? She might get a job on the wharf, but that's hard labor. Conor is young and able, but he doesn't have the best history with his family and there aren't going to be too many places that are flexible with his school schedule. I resent that you can just come here and turn so many lives upside down without a second thought."

"You have got to be kidding me. My aunt isn't the only person who has owned a business and has died. This happens all the time," I say. I know I sound heartless, but the fact that she is blaming me for three people losing their jobs is just ridiculous. "I'm sorry that this affects your family, but this affects me, too. I didn't ask for any of this." I get up to leave because now I'm just pissed off, but she grabs my forearm.

"Grace, wait. You haven't even heard all of it." I'm very much aware of her fingers still curled around my arm so instead of jerking my arm out of her grasp and further embarrassing both of us, I stop and lean against the bar.

"There's more? What else? Are you going to blame me for every break up because now Howth doesn't have a flower shop and people can't send flowers as an apology? I've heard enough, Kerry. Thanks for the beer." I head for the exit, grabbing my coat on the way out. The biting wind feels good against my heated body. I don't even know why my aunt wanted me to work with the Mulligans. Kerry is not a nice person. Admirable that she cares for her family and the other people who work there, but completely ridiculous in blaming me. I head the way we came, hoping to get lost in the crowd. I have no idea where I am, but I know there is a rail station close by. I follow the signs until I see the station and buy a one way ticket back to Howth. Screw her. She can just earn her commission by coming out to the shop when she needs me to sign papers.

CHAPTER FIVE

The bedroom is the hardest room for me to go through, which is probably the reason I save it for last. My bedroom is my sanctuary and judging by the large envelope of letters and mementos I find in the closet, it was hers, too. A letter addressed to me is on the floor by the nightstand. I guess Abram knocked it over or the wind did when Kerry opened the windows to air out the rooms. I open it with great anticipation, hoping for answers that nobody in my family has for me.

Gracie,

I hope that you remember me and the little time we spent together years ago. I remember you fondly and our talk at your grandfather's retirement. It made the biggest impact on my life. I am sure you are curious as to why you are my beneficiary. Believe it or not, you talked me into being true to my heart and to myself as you were struggling with dealing with your own sexuality. You were open with me, but worried about how your family would take it. I was worried about the same thing for myself, but you helped me make the decision to follow my heart and be with my true love. By now hopefully you've found pictures of me and Kate. I followed her to Ireland, but kept my distance until I realized I was hurting both of us. When I finally told her my true feelings, we had ten remarkable years together. Those were the best years of my life and I have you to thank for them. We had been friends for years, but seeing your strength and determination to be true to yourself, I decided to take a chance and reveal my feelings to Kate. Thankfully, she reciprocated and we had a beautiful life together until she passed away two years ago. I was never close to anyone in the family. With your love for art and beauty, I wanted you to have an opportunity to get away from your life in Texas and start fresh somewhere else. If this isn't something you want, then please sell the shop and use the money for a fabulous vacation or to do something you've always wanted.

I hope you appreciate our little shop. We've done a lot of good in this town and people respect it. They never questioned my relationship with Kate and accepted us with open arms. They have wonderful hearts and I hope that you spend some time here so that you can experience the kindness and love we did. Thank you, Grace, for your enlightenment years ago.

Always,
Nola

Kerry's business card is attached to the letter. Apparently, Aunt Nola saw something in Kerry that I've only caught a glimpse of. Didn't she know how obstinate Kerry is? Stubborn just grazes Kerry's surface. In the short time I've known her, she has managed to annoy me to the point where I don't even want to talk to her again. I wouldn't mind looking at her from a good distance, but no words. Her hair fascinates me. Is it always wavy and does it feel as thick as it looks? No. I don't care. And her full lips. Are they as soft as they look? I shake my head, trying to rid the image of her from my mind. I'm mad at her for laying a guilt trip on me for something I don't have control over. Was she this rude to my aunt? Probably not since my aunt was still employing her family and friends. My heart feels heavy from this day. I head for the kitchen to fix tea. That will get rid of the chill and maybe even settle me down. I pick up Abram and pet him while the water heats up. He's the perfect cat for a family with children. He doesn't care that I pick him up, flip him on his back, and rub his belly. He sprawls out and purrs as I pet him. I'm going to miss him when I leave. The tea kettle whistles that the water is ready, and for the first time since I got here, I sit down and relax. I have a warm cup of peppermint tea and a lovable cat as my company. I'm at peace.

I wake up to Abram leaving my arms and jumping off of the couch. Apparently, I was tired because we've been asleep for at least two hours. There is something about this place and this cat that makes me want to nap all of the time. I look around the room and freeze when I see Kerry squatting down in the doorway, petting Abram.

"What are you doing here?" I ask, my defenses instantly up.

"I came to apologize," she says. I'm completely unnerved at her in my space and I'm wavering between telling her to get out and telling her to have a seat. I don't like it when people watch me sleep. Not that I think she was because it doesn't appear that she's been here long, but it still is unsettling. She shrugs out of her overcoat and gently places it across the back of the chair. Picking up Abram, she nuzzles him for a few seconds before sitting in the chair and plopping him on her lap. I slide up into a sitting position and rub my hands over my face in an effort to wake up. "Look, Grace, I'm not an easy person to get to know and our initial meeting wasn't great, but I still have no right to get upset with you." I reach out and hand her the letter. I'm just tired of arguing and being on edge around her. I need space so I head for the kitchen and rinse out my cup of tea. Now I'm just hungry. I'm sure if I head back to the bed and breakfast, Ms. Walsh will whip me up something to eat even though it's between lunch and dinner.

"This is an incredibly sweet letter from your aunt. I guess I never knew that your family had such a hard time with it," she says.

"Yeah, at least my mom supported me. I'm not very close to the rest of my family. Now I understand things a lot better and why Aunt Nola left everything to me. I never knew this about her," I say. I'm a mixture of sad and angry at my aunt for not sharing with me, but on some level, I understand her hesitancy to share such private information. When you're young and coming out, people are more inclined to support you because you're just learning about sex and your attractions. It's got to be easier than when you are in your forties or fifties and coming to that realization.

"I knew about Kate only because Emma's been working here for about eight years. I never got the chance to meet her though," she says, still holding the letter. I watch as she rereads the letter, her fingers playing with her bottom lip, drawing my attention to its fullness. I'm struck with an urge to pull her close to me, touch her, kiss her. That strong desire confuses me and I head back into the kitchen. I can't be attracted to her. Nothing good can come from it. She follows me.

"I know I haven't been agreeable or even nice. My mother would be so disappointed in my behavior toward you. It's just an unfortunate event that Nola passed away, for everybody involved." I can hear the sadness in her voice so I know she's being truthful. I see her chest rise and fall with a deep breath she inhales and holds before exhaling. When she looks up at me, I see resolution in her eyes. "I really am sorry. Let me take you to dinner. I ruined your lunch so the least I can do is treat you to a nice meal." I have no reason to say no, plus I'm starving. If Aunt Nola thinks we should work together, I need to at least give her a chance.

"I would like that. And I'm hungry." She laughs at my honesty, her laughter light and infectious. It's a lovely sound. I excuse myself for a few minutes to freshen up. I finger brush my hair and braid it back. I'll be wearing a hat anyway so it really doesn't matter. It's amazing to me how much everybody walks around here. I splash some water on my face to wake up and pinch my cheeks for color.

"What are you hungry for?" she asks when I return to the living room. I bite my tongue from spewing out something lewd and shrug.

"Anything really. I haven't eaten since breakfast."

"Is there anything you won't eat? I know a lot of Americans are vegetarians." I smile at her.

"I live in Texas. It's practically the beef capital of the United States. I'll eat just about anything."

"We eat a lot of fish, mutton, and chicken. My mother makes the best mutton stew in the world," she says, grabbing her coat. I'm disappointed when her body disappears underneath it. I was enjoying her curves.

"I've had fish and chips twice now so maybe something a little bit different," I say.

"Well, then I have the perfect place for us," she says. I follow her out and lock up, knowing I won't be back here until tomorrow. I need to get back to the bed and breakfast before Ms. Walsh forgets I'm a boarder. I slip into the car and notice it's different than the one Luke left for her.

"Is this a rental?" I ask. She holds out her hands in a surrendering gesture.

"Let's just forget about that, at least for tonight," she says. I nod and look outside at the darkening sky.

"Is it going to rain?"

"It always rains. At least for a little bit." She eases out onto the street and within about twenty minutes we are parked outside a solitary restaurant on top of a foothill, Dublin's blinking lights off in the distance.

"Wow, this is really a nice place, Kerry. Am I even dressed appropriately?" I ask, suddenly self-conscious at my jeans and sweater.

"You look fine. This is one of my favorite restaurants and I don't get the opportunity to come here very often," she says. We are seated next to a window that overlooks the Irish countryside. It's too bad that it's not lighter out because I'm sure the view is breathtaking. She orders us a bottle of wine and sits back in her chair. This Kerry I could get used to. "So, tell me about yourself, Grace."

"I work. That's about it," I say. My mind wanders back to an e-mail I read this morning about one of our accounts. My team is more than capable of making decisions without me, but nobody wants to pull the trigger. Even thousands of miles away, I'm still holding their hands. She scoffs.

"I know there is more to you than just work. What are your hobbies? What is your favorite thing about Texas? Are you dating anyone?" That last question perks me up.

"I really work six or seven days a week. This is my first vacation in about three years. I love the Texas weather because it's almost always warm and no, I'm not dating anyone." I take a drink of wine, surprised at how relaxed I am. This wine will put me under the table. I need to limit myself.

"I've never been to America. I've been all across Europe and a few countries in Africa," she says.

"You've been to more countries than I have. I went to Mexico with my best friend Morgan once and France when I graduated college. As a matter of fact, I was afraid my passport expired and I wouldn't be able to get out here quickly, but I still have a year left on it." The server arrives to take our orders and Kerry asks if she can order for me. She's definitely a take charge kind of woman and I find that I like it. She orders meatloaf with cabbage cream sauce and Colcannon, a potato and cabbage side dish.

"I have a feeling I'm going to put on at least ten pounds while I am here," I say.

"Well, I'm certain that won't hurt you," she says. I snort thinking I've got her beat by at least that. I smile a thank you. She continues the conversation talking about food, traveling, and all the different things she's tasted. I find her quite charming when she doesn't act like she hates me. By the time the meal is served, we've finished one bottle of wine and I've learned all about her twin brother and the pranks they played on each other growing up. They are close now, but that wasn't always the case.

"I thought your brother was super sweet at the pub," I say.

She laughs. "Yeah, that's what he wants you to think. He's very charming around pretty girls, especially blondes." She's complimented me three times since we sat down. We start the second bottle of wine and I have to remind myself not to flirt with her, regardless of her compliments.

"I have an older brother," I say. "And Morgan is the closest thing I have to a sister."

"She's your best friend, right?"

"Yes. She was actually supposed to accompany me here, but she fractured her ankle two days before we were scheduled to fly out so I came out alone. I'm so glad I did because she would have been too bored to go through all of Aunt Nola's stuff with me. She would have stayed in Dublin and chased after all the available women," I say.

"She's a lesbian, too? Did you ever date?" Kerry asks.

"Oh, no. She's too much for me to handle. Stubborn and very high-maintenance. I just don't have the energy for that. We agreed a long time ago to just stay friends," I say.

"So, you don't like a challenge?" she asks.

"Depends on the challenge." Suddenly, I am flirting with her, but after almost two bottles of wine, I just don't care. The waitress shows up with our food before I have a chance to continue our playful banter. The food smells divine and I heartily dig in. I moan with appreciation at the combined flavors. "This is fantastic! How do you manage to stay so thin?" I take an even bigger bite.

"I'm single so I don't eat like this every day. If I did, I'm sure I'd be the size of a house," she says.

"Why are you still single?" I ask.

"Apparently I am too much of a challenge," she says. I bust out laughing. Beautiful with a hearty sense of humor.

"So tell me what you didn't get to tell me when I rudely stormed out of the bar," I say. A look of sadness flashes across her face.

"When I said I wasn't being fair to you, I meant that. I'm mad at myself, too, Grace. I'm a hypocrite." She pauses, takes a drink of water, and continues explaining. "I'm upset because when you sell the shop, I get a fantastic commission check that will allow me to have a down payment for the farm I've dreamed about. So you win, I win, and the people I love lose." She leans back in her chair, defeated. "So you see, I'm quite a mess over this. I'm trying to find a way to deal with it, but instead I have only been mean to you. So from here on out, I promise to only be a friend."

"I will gladly hold you to that."

Chapter Six

I surprise myself by getting most of Aunt Nola's stuff either packed up or put in an organized pile for the thrift store. I don't even know if Ireland has something like thrift stores. I'll be sure to ask Leigh when she arrives today. I told Leigh, Emma, and Conor that The Irish Garden will continue to operate until it sells. I also told them that if they needed time to look for a job, we could shut down early on days they might have an interview lined up. I just don't know how things are done over here. They seem appreciative that I'm not closing it down right away. Last night, Kerry told me that I will probably have all three employees there until the very end. Emma will have the baby within a few weeks and then go on parental leave for twenty-six weeks. At least the government will help out with some expenses while she is getting accustomed to motherhood. I feel like I should offer some sort of severance package to them and might do that if the sale goes off without a hitch. I'm sure that's what Aunt Nola would have wanted me to do with some of the money.

I decide to call Morgan and check in with her. "Where have you been?" she answers, knowing it's me.

"I'm doing great. How are you? How's the ankle?" I ask.

"Sorry. Hi. How are you? How's the sale going?" she asks.

"I'm glad I added on a week because now I'm not so rushed. I found some important photos and letters to my family that I have already boxed up and will send to my condo. The rest of her stuff I will offer it as either part of the sale or ask if the employees want anything. Her stuff is very cool. Retro and very clean," I say. "The clothes I will donate somewhere. If they don't have a thrift store around here, I'm sure one of the many churches have a charity program."

"So when will you be back in the office?" Morgan asks.

"I'm not sure really." I cringe waiting for Morgan's reaction.

"Don't worry about us. For the most part, the team is getting along without you," she says. I notice that she is not copied on a lot of the e-mails. I'm unsettled about that. My team knows better, especially since I am not there.

"I've heard from a few people," I say.

"I'm sure they were told to reach out to you only if it's an emergency. They know you haven't had a vacation in a long time," she says. "So tell me more. Last time we spoke, nobody at the flower shop liked you, and the hot real estate agent wanted to kill you. Please tell me things are better."

"Thankfully, I worked it out with Kerry. We actually had a nice dinner together last night," I say. I feel the smile cross my face as I think about our evening.

"Ooh. Well, that sounds promising," she says.

"So, you are not going to believe this. My aunt was a lesbian. Had a lover and everything. That's the whole reason why she left everything to me. At the retirement party I told her all about me and what I was going through with my family. Hang on, let me read you her letter." I dig out the letter and read it to Morgan, answering her questions as she interrupts me.

"That's so wonderful, Grace. You helped your aunt follow her heart. Love doesn't get any better than that," she says. "So now it's up to you to find love. Or at least get hooked up with a lass." Her Irish brogue is horrible and sounds more English, but I let it slide.

"I'll take this weekend off and I'm sure I'll find a gay bar in Dublin," I say. We talk a few minutes more about work before Morgan has to get off of the phone.

"Try to unwind while you are there. The photos you've e-mailed me are gorgeous. You need to take a few days and explore."

"Well, I will need a guide because I'm not driving here. Even if I didn't cause Kerry to crash, I still wouldn't want to get behind the wheel."

"You are such a puss," she says. This I know. We say our good-byes and I make my way downstairs. I hear voices so I know the store is open.

"Good morning," I say. I'm surprised to see Kerry here. I glance down and realize I'm going to have to do laundry since I'm wearing the same jeans from last night. Now that I've decided to extend my stay, I might as well stay in my aunt's apartment. At least I can wash my clothes here.

"Grace, I have a few more papers for you to sign if you have about ten minutes." Today she is a bit more casual, wearing slacks and a sweater. Suddenly, I'm very self-conscious.

"Sure. We can either squeeze into the office here or go upstairs," I say.

"The office should be fine." She follows me into the back of the shop.

"I can't believe we didn't get everything signed at your office," I say. I offer her a cup of coffee which she accepts. I definitely like this agreeable and relaxed side of her.

"Since you want to sell the place with a furnished apartment, I had to add the extra value into the listing price. It won't take you long." She has placed tiny arrow stickers on the pages I'm supposed to sign and I find myself skittish with her this close to me. Out of my peripheral vision, I can see her staring at me, her eyes focusing on my face. I'm glad that I took time to apply a little bit of makeup when I woke up today. "I had fun last night,

Grace. I'm glad we buried the hatchet." I turn to smile at her and am unnerved that she has moved more into my personal space. She's almost close enough kiss. I can't help that my eyes dart down to her full lips and again, I am struck with the urge to kiss her. I lean back a bit, not enough to let her know her closeness is affecting me, but enough to let my heart stop beating so fast. When she reaches down and points to something on the page, an errant curl slides down her arm and brushes softly against my arm. I suppress a shudder. "Don't forget to initial right here." Her voice is low, her breath warm against my neck. What is happening to me? Just twenty-four hours ago, I wanted nothing to do with her. Now I feel like I'm crushing on her. In my defense, though, she is far more attractive when she isn't scowling at me.

"There. That should do it." I hand the papers back to her and take a safe step back. She has to know she's affecting me. She smiles and files the papers back into her bag. "I will send our photographer out to take photos of the place if you are ready."

"Oh, I can take photos. I have my cameras with me," I say, getting excited at the possibility of helping in this process. She looks at me warily. I hold up my hand. "Let me take them and if you don't like them, you can bring your photographer in. This is what I do, Kerry. I get paid to make things look great and sell."

"Okay, but I will be critical and we need to get it done soon so that we can have it listed by the time you leave," she says.

"I do need your help with the upstairs. I want to donate my aunt's clothes to either a thrift store or a church. Is that something you can help me with? Or do thrift stores come out and pick things up?"

"Well, I think you mean a charity store and we would have to take your aunt's clothes there. That shouldn't take but a trip or two. Do you already have it all divided up?" she asks.

"Almost. I ran out of the bags Leigh and Emma found for me down here," I say.

"I can either bring some by later or I can take you out if you would like," she says.

"It's no bother. If you tell me where the closest place is, I can just walk to it," I say.

"Grace, we're friends now. This is what friends do for one another. Of course, if you want, you can drive your aunt's car," she says. She smiles and I know she's teasing. I've made it clear that I would never drive here.

"No. I'm good. Walking is good for me," I say. She doesn't have to know that I drive everywhere back home. Even to the quaint neighborhood ice cream shop that is only four short blocks from my condo.

"You know, this is a pretty good town to learn how to drive in. It's not too busy, besides most people are already at work. You do know how to drive a standard, right?" I waiver for a bit, then wave my hands side to side.

"No, no. Really. I'll walk," I say.

"Well, I'm not doing anything. Let me help you and then we can at least get this part done. It will be a lot easier to take photos without tons of bags in your way," she says. Kerry does have a good point. I finally concede and follow her out to her car.

"I'm pretty sure you have plenty of work to do today that doesn't involve me," I say. "And I'm not trying to be rude. I just know you work hard and hanging out with me isn't making you money. Trust me, I know all about time management."

"It's Friday. There isn't anything going on. At least I haven't received any calls yet so no worries," she says.

"How is the market here in Ireland?" I've noticed quite a few for sale signs in yards and in storefronts. She shrugs.

"It's not great. I got into the family business right when the housing market crashed, about eight years ago. It's been an uphill battle ever since. Dublin has bounced back quite well, but most of Ireland is still struggling," she says.

"Have you always wanted to get involved in real estate?"

"Oh, no. I went to college for a few years to become an agriculturist. Then when the family business started failing, I knew I needed to help out. I've been a part of the Mulligan group ever since." Her smile is a sad smile.

"Well, I'm sure you're successful," I say. She's a beautiful woman with a ton of spirit. I can't imagine people not falling all over themselves to give her business.

"I do okay. It helps that I live at home still. Remember, I'm saving up for the farm," she says. I giggle. She doesn't strike me as the farming type.

"Really? I see you more as a cosmopolitan girl. Someone who needs the big city in order to thrive," I say. She laughs.

"I live in the city now and have most of my life. You can live ten kilometers outside of the city limits and it seems like you've been transported five hundred years back in time. I like the solitude and the privacy of a little bit of land."

"Huh." She floors me with her plan. "So what kind of crops would you have on your farm?" I'm so proud of myself for not smiling during that delivery.

"Barley and other things. I don't want a big place, but just enough to keep me busy."

"You should come to Texas and see the farms we have. You could not pick two different places on earth," I say. "Does it get very warm here?"

"What's warm to you?" she asks. I pull out my phone to convert my one hundred degree Fahrenheit days into Celsius.

"Well, most of our summers are thirty seven degrees Celsius," I say.

"No! That can't be right. Maybe when we have a very hot summer, we might hit thirty once or twice, but usually we stay around twenty," she says. I quickly do the conversions and find that most of the summers here are in the upper sixties, lower seventies.

"Do you ever swim?"

"Of course. Maybe we are just used to the weather here. I would melt if I lived in Texas. What about the winters?" she asks. We spend the rest of the drive to the store and back discussing the weather. Texas winters are similar to Irish summers. Kerry parks and follows me into the shop. There are a few customers inside ordering flowers for an upcoming birthday party. She stops a moment to say hello to both patrons. I watch her interact with them. She's extremely friendly and focused on them. I can tell she genuinely cares. This is why she's successful at her job. Knowing that I'm staring and it's starting to get awkward, I signal to her that I'm headed upstairs and she nods. She holds my gaze for just a fraction longer than normal and I feel a flush of warmth push through my veins. I need to curb this crush I'm developing. Morgan's right. I need to find an available Irish girl, get my kiss, and get out of town.

Chapter Seven

"Wow. All of these bags are going to the charity store?" I'm just about done bagging up Nola's clothes, leaving out the warm coats that I will donate to her church.

"Have you changed your mind about helping me?" I ask.

"No, but I will be right back," she says, disappearing again. I move all the bags closer to the door and am surprised when Kerry returns with Conor. Without even asking, he scoops up several of the bags and heads down the stairs.

"I could have done it," I say. Kerry waves me off.

"I know, but why when we have a young, strapping lad here who is more than willing to help us?" She does have a point. We make two trips down to Kerry's car and The Irish Garden's delivery van. Conor is taking over a load so that we can be done in a single drive to the charity store. "Now you can spend a little time for yourself and do some sightseeing things. You've been here a week and what do you know about Ireland? What have you seen other than three hours at the harbor here in town? The DART will only take you so far. Since you aren't comfortable driving and since you don't want me to drive you around, you should look into hiring a driver to take you around. Ireland is a beautiful place and I know you don't take a lot of vacations. Go south and visit the Blarney Castle or go to the other side of Ireland and see the Cliffs of Moher."

"I feel guilty that you're driving me around. I'm not your responsibility." I want to tell her that I'm her client and I'm not really relaxed around her, but I keep my response short. "You have a job to do. Other clients need you. You don't need to drive me around." It doesn't escape me that her phone keeps chiming. "I might take a bus tour to the other side. That sounds like fun." I see her roll her eyes and bite her cheek to keep herself from getting upset. I smile knowing this is hard for her.

"It's not a problem for me. Today is Friday. How about you take pics of your aunt's place and I will come by on Sunday, my official day off, to collect the photos and then we will go see a few castles. It's supposed to be a nice, warm day. You have all of this camera equipment and nothing to take photos of." She tsks like she's scolding a child. I sigh.

"Okay, but only if you have time," I say. My mouth is dry at the thought of spending an entire day with her. I make a mental note to stay away from alcohol.

"I'll have my car back tomorrow, so it will be a more comfortable ride," she says.

"Luke needs to bill me. I haven't seen anything on my card yet."

"Oh, I'm sure he will." She pulls in front of The Irish Garden to let me out. "I'll see you on Sunday. How about nine? I'll pick you up at the Walsh. We can grab breakfast before we head out."

"I'm staying here the rest of my trip," I say. Her eyes widen in surprise.

"That's a great idea. Okay, then, nine Sunday morning."

I nod and wave thanks for all of her help today.

❖

Abram is not camera shy. He follows me to every room. I have deleted several photos already because his tail or his ear ends up in the shot. I'm not upset. It makes me laugh. He's confused and can't figure out why I'm climbing on chairs and couches so he has to billy goat his way right next to me. I scratch behind his ears and above his tail and smile as he purrs at me. I'm going to miss this little lovable guy. I slip on my boots and jacket so I can go outside and take photos of the front of the shop. I wait until the sun shines through the clouds and head across the street. This time I pay attention to the traffic both ways. After snapping several shots, I head back inside and boot up my computer to upload the photos. I'm pleased with them. I can't imagine Kerry wanting different ones. I dig up a flash drive and copy them over, hoping she uses the majority of them.

Conor has offered to help take my boxes to the post office so that I can get them out of the shop. I know filling out all of the paperwork is going to take forever so we head up there with all nine boxes.

"I can pick you up in an hour if you need me to," he says. "It's no problem. I will get most of the deliveries done before noon." I understand why my aunt hired him. He's a sweet young man and a very hard worker. He's the first to help out carrying things for us and others around. Today his usual moppy hair is tucked into a beanie type hat to keep him warm. There isn't much heat in the van because of the flowers, but just enough to keep the chill away.

"I'm sure by the time I'm done, the sun will be warm and my walk will be enjoyable. You go do what you need to. Just giving me a ride to the post office is so helpful."

"You won't recognize where you are tomorrow. It's supposed to be a warm day. The perfect Sunday. Different than today. If you don't like the weather here in Ireland, wait a day," he says, his crooked smile infectious. Yeah, everybody in the world says that about their weather, but I just smile back at him.

I'm surprised that the post office is just up the street from the flower shop, so the drive lasts only a minute or two. Thankfully, no patrons are inside because I know I'm going to need a lot of time and attention. I assure Conor that I will be fine and shoo him away. I know he has to study this weekend and still has deliveries to make today. The clerks are friendly and help me with the forms. They speak of Aunt Nola fondly and again I am surprised at how many people knew her. It only takes me thirty minutes until I'm done with the boxes. It's noon and I have the entire day and night to play. My aunt's apartment is completely cleaned out and I feel a huge relief wash over me. I was premature in extending my trip, so I can at least play tourist now and head out to see some of this beautiful country. Conor told me of one to two day bus tours that will take me over to the other side of the island. Today I'll load up my cameras and take the DART to Dublin. There is entirely too much to see and I've rushed both times I've been in the city. Today will be different. I will take my time and enjoy my afternoon.

By the time the train gets me into the heart of Dublin, I'm hungry. I check out places around to eat on TripAdvisor.com and pick Darkey Kelly's, a pub with excellent food and great atmosphere, according to the reviews. I'm more comfortable going into restaurants alone now and enter it without trepidation. I find a booth and a waitress zips over to me, menu in hand. I order a crab sandwich and a goat cheese with beetroot salad. Since it's early in the day, I stick with beer and order an Irish Red. Instantly, I think of Kerry and her deep auburn hair. I want to see her hair completely down, the long waves framing her face and cascading down her back. Most of the time, it is pulled back with a ribbon, or some type of updo. I wonder what she is doing today. I wonder if she is thinking about me, too. Now that we've supposedly buried the hatchet and are cautiously approaching a friendship, I don't feel as guilty thinking about her. I allow my thoughts to linger on her perfect skin, the way she tilts her head when she laughs, and how good she is with her family. I understand why she's upset about all of this. I sigh and finish my beer. The waitress is quick to bring me another. She asks if I want dessert, but I want to check out a bakery down the street so I politely refuse and ask for the check instead.

I head out and get lost in the Dublin crowd. Weekends in the city are very popular and since the weather has improved since this morning, a lot of people are out. I spend time at Trinity College and I get a glimpse of my first castle, Dublin Castle. I'm disappointed that it doesn't look like a medieval castle, but snap a ton of pictures of it anyway. It is, after all, my first. I see a rainbow flag displayed outside of a bar and head over to check it out. A cute girl is standing by the door passing out flyers.

"Come to the auction tonight," she says, slipping a pink flyer into my hand.

"What kind of auction is it?"

"At eight tonight, several available bachelorettes in Dublin are going to be auctioned off for a date with the highest bidder. All proceeds go to the BeLonG To LGBT community in Dublin. This is the fifth year. It would be great to see you here later."

I nod and slip the flyer into my back pocket. This sounds like fun on all sorts of levels. It's only four o'clock. I need to get back to my aunt's, freshen up, eat something and then come back. I've done enough sightseeing for one day. The night is for relaxing. And women. Definitely women.

❖

"So, ladies, remember this is for a good cause. I want to see a lot of euros up here on this stage!" The MC of the event, who also happens to be the owner of the bar, doesn't need a microphone. Her voice booms over the loud crowd and I hear her before I see her. I have walked into a bar of Irish lesbians. The smile on my face couldn't be any bigger.

"Here. Compliments of the bar and me." A shot of dark liquid is thrust into my hand, the deliverer half drunk and very cute. She's about six inches from my face and I think she is going to kiss me, but she leans back, clinks her glass to mine, and shoots the liquid instead. Her eyes are closed, the smile on her face dreamy. I love happy drunk people. She waits until I finish my drink. "Carry on!" She dances away from me and heads back to her friends. I lick my lips, the spicy liquor strong and not unpleasant. I see an empty stool at the bar and make a beeline toward it. This will be my perch for the rest of the evening. I can see the stage from here and I have liquor within my reach. Not to mention I'm surrounded by beautiful women who are all in a good mood.

"On the house." The bartender, probably the only man here, slides another drink in front of me. He winks and disappears to help a waitress fill orders. If this keeps up, I won't have to buy any drinks tonight. I turn my attention to the stage and watch as bachelorette number three is up for grabs. She's cute and spunky with short, dark hair. The bidding starts at twenty euros and it's up to one hundred in no time. I'm half tempted to join in the bidding, but my shyness wins out and I stay seated and watch instead. I don't think I've ever had this much fun back home, especially by myself. Two women are in a bidding war and the crowd is going wild. I hope the rest of the bachelorettes get this much attention. I promise myself if they don't, I will step in. That's the whiskey talking. I can feel its warmth spread throughout my body. The tips of my fingers tingle, and my lips are very sensitive and feel warm. The bachelorette is sold for a whopping two hundred and twenty euros. The bar erupts with whistles, laughter, and applause.

"We've set the bar, ladies. Let's bring out bachelorette number four. A well-known attorney in Dublin whose hobbies include horseback riding, hiking, and women. Lots of women." More whooping and hollering. I see a few women scowling so I figure this gorgeous woman on stage has broken a few hearts around here. I signal for another drink, something lighter, and anxiously await the bidding. Her number is already at two hundred euros and they aren't slowing down.

"C'mon, Kerry. How about you join in on the bidding since you won't let us auction you off?" The MC interrupts the party when a group of three women enter the bar. The crowd, including myself, turns to look at the new patrons and I literally slide off my stool when I see Kerry, my Kerry, standing in the doorway, flanked by two gorgeous women. She pauses slightly when we make eye contact, and continues her trek through the crowd, heading right for me, waving off the MC in the process. I feel like a deer in headlights, nothing to do but watch as she struts right toward me. I blink at her in surprise when she is a few feet in front of me. I gulp down the rest of my fourth whiskey, slamming the empty glass a little bit harder than I intended. I blame my warbled perception.

"Well, well, well. What a surprise," I say. A smile spreads deliciously across her face and I fight the strong desire to press myself to her. Realizing I'm in her personal space, I casually lean back and try to hop back up onto the stool. My leather jacket that I've been sitting on slides me right off and not very gracefully. Before I plop down on the floor, Kerry grabs my arm and holds me up. I giggle.

"Are you enjoying our fine whiskey?" she asks after helping me back onto the stool. Her fingers are warm and strong against my bare arm. I can feel chill bumps gathering under her grip. I gently pull away, pretending to right myself and needing both of my hands. I don't want her to know she's affecting me.

"Hey, Kerry. We've got a table up front and left of the stage. Come find us when…" her friend pauses, not quite sure how to handle our interaction. "Umm…just come find us." She nods at them and turns her attention back to me.

"I see you found this place," she says. She leans over me to order drinks for her friends. She smells cold like the outside even though I can feel her body heat radiating off of her. They must have walked here.

"Who are your friends?" I ask. "They are very pretty."

"Well, what am I?" The Kerry in front of me is confident and smooth, slightly cocky. My crush just got bigger.

"You're beautiful. How did I not know about you?" She raises her eyebrow at me.

"I look the same," she says. I laugh. "How many drinks have you had tonight?" she asks. I smile. I think I even giggle again.

"Tom, how many drinks have I had?" Tom is somewhere behind the bar. I don't know if he hears me, but I see Kerry nod at someone behind me. I don't care enough to turn around. "I don't know. A cute girl gave me a drink when I first got here. And then Tom let me try different Irish whiskeys. I didn't think I liked whiskey, but it is actually quite tasty." I lick my lips and smack them, the numbness disturbing. I bite my bottom lip to feel something and am completely surprised when Kerry reaches out and runs her thumb on my lip. My whole body explodes with instant heat as my body responds to her touch.

"Don't. You don't want to bleed." Her voice is low and she is close enough for me to feel her breath on my face.

"You know, when you whisper or talk low, you don't sound so stiff. I've noticed the Irish always sound like they have important business even when they are talking about simple things like the weather." She throws her head back and laughs.

"That's about right, Grace. Come. Join us up front. It's more exciting." She grabs her drinks and nods in the direction for me to follow.

"It's okay. I'm good here. Thank you though. I don't want to move around much," I say.

"Order some greasy food. That will help," she says. "Don't overdo it on the whiskey, however good it might be." She winks and leaves me. I'm bummed because I thought she would put up more of a fight to get me to hang with them. I watch her lithe form walk away and get swallowed up by the crowd.

"Tom, I'm going to need something to drink," I say. He slides a water in front of me. "Can I chase this with a Jameson?"

"Yeah, Tom, give her a Jameson. My treat." Bachelorette number three is in front of me. She spins my chair a bit so that my legs are trapped between hers. This night just got really interesting. I beg that Morgan's confidence channels through me.

"Aren't you supposed to be on a date?" I ask. Her smile is beautiful.

"An American! Even better. My date had to make a phone call. What brings you to Dublin?" I explain my situation in as few words as possible. She hands me my Jameson and clinks my glass. "Cheers to your aunt." She follows that with a toast in Gaelic that I calmly sit and wait for her to finish because I don't understand any of it. It sounds beautiful and her accent is crisp and pleasant. "So, are you staying nearby?" I'm sure that's not a pick up line and she is genuinely interested in my business.

"Tom, can I get a beer?" I stifle a shiver as Kerry is suddenly behind me, signaling for the bartender.

"Kerry." The bachelorette whose name either escapes me or was never shared looks Kerry up and down and takes a step back from me. A slight frown bows down the corners of her mouth. These two women know one another and their relationship isn't all rainbows and butterflies.

"Donna. I trust you are doing well," Kerry says. She almost dismisses her, turning her attention back to Tom, signing her receipt. This looks juicy. I can actually feel the tension between them.

"Donna," I say for no apparent reason. Both women look at me. I smile for no apparent reason. Christ, I'm drunk. "I couldn't remember if you told me your name."

"Yes. This is Donna Winslow. We've known each other since secondary school," Kerry explains. She cocks her head to the side and blinks. Oh, man, this definitely is not a good relationship. I want to know more.

"Oh, so you went to the same school?" I ask. I feel like a director of a soap opera, my view bouncing back and forth between them as words are shared.

"Something like that," Donna says. She casually looks down at her nails as if she is bored, but even drunk I can see Donna is slightly shaking with an underlying anger.

"We liked to date the same girls. In Donna's case, at the same time, unbeknownst to me," Kerry says, matter-of-factly. "Not once, but twice." I can't understand why Donna is the mad one here. Kerry is surprisingly calm. Definitely different than the Kerry I met eight days ago. The one who was full of fire and beautiful anger.

"That wasn't very nice," I say, turning my attention to Donna.

"Oh, I'm over it. Those girls weren't worth it," Kerry says. She's holding her drinks, but not leaving.

"That wasn't very nice," I say, this time to Kerry.

"Are you sure you don't want to sit with us?" This time I waiver. I don't want to upset Kerry, regardless of how attractive I find Donna. Our new relationship is too important.

"Sure. I would love to." Donna takes a step back, allowing me to slip off of my chair.

"Thanks for the drink." I shrug at Donna, disappointed that I'm walking away from my possibly one and only opportunity to hook up. Kerry introduces me to her friends and slides a chair next to her. I sit down and am instantly alert when her body brushes mine. I feel my heart hammering in every soft part of me, the fast thumping swelling my body with need. I thought this would be easier. My body is betraying me. It's the damn whiskey. I won't last here much longer. By the seventh bachelorette, I turn to Kerry and tell her I don't feel well and need some air. I quickly stand up and grab my coat and head for the door before she even has a chance to respond.

The cold air swirls around me, calming my heat and my heart. I slip my leather jacket on and head for the train station. If the trains aren't running, I'll just take a cab back to my aunt's. I'm no longer drunk, but sufficiently tipsy. At least I'm upright and thinking straight.

"Where are you even going?" I hear behind me. I turn to find Kerry walking quickly toward me.

"I just need space. I don't feel the greatest," I say. I find that my body has refused to move and I wait for her to catch up to me.

"Well, you don't need to be out alone," she says, the reprimanding tone in her voice causes my anger to surface.

"I'm in the city on a popular street. Nothing's going to happen to me." I take a step back when she gets close to me.

"You are a tourist in a new city in a different country. You sound and look American. Too many people out here will try to take advantage of you," she says. I smile slowly at her, thoughts of Irish women hanging on me fill my head. "What's so funny?"

"Well, that doesn't sound half bad. Tonight was going to be my night, you know," I say.

"What do you mean?"

"I was going to kiss an Irish girl. That was the one thing I wanted to do and tonight was probably my only chance," I say.

"You're mad that I interrupted you and Donna? She's a snake, Grace. She is not somebody you want to know personally," Kerry says. She steps closer to me. I take a step back.

"You do not know me that well, Kerry. I'm leaving in a week, perhaps even sooner since most of my aunt's affairs have been taken care of."

"You should stay," she says, taking another step closer, this time to make room for a couple walking by us. My back is up against the wall. I can feel the cold bricks through my jeans.

"Why? You barely tolerate me," I say. It's more of a mumble because I don't really believe it.

"I thought we were friends now," she says. Now she's smiling. She knows I'm trapped. She takes a step closer. She's in my personal space. Even with my boots on, I have to look up at her. I tilt my head back and gasp when she reaches down and curls her hands around the opening of either side of my jacket. She pulls me toward her, closing the gap. I don't protest. Her lips capture mine in a searing kiss and I whimper with a mixture of delight, need, and submission. Kerry's mouth is warm, wet, and her tongue soft against my lips. I open up to the kiss, suck her tongue into my mouth and kiss her back with a need that surprises me. By the time we break apart, we are both breathing heavily and clutching one another. I don't think either one of us expected that. She takes a step back from me to steady herself. She releases the grip on my jacket and smoothes down the crumpled leather, not realizing that her fingers are brushing my breasts. I can't help but shiver and she stops when she recognizes what she's doing. "Umm. Let me take you home." I raise my eyebrow at her. "Back to the shop. It will be safer." Somehow, I don't think so.

"No. Stay with your friends. I'll just take a cab," I say. I hope I come across as casual as I'm trying to be.

"Let's go," she says. "We aren't far from my place. I'll get my car and take you home." I feel like sulking. I wish we could have just ended the night with that fantastic kiss. We don't say much on our way back to the car. Kerry asks a few questions about my day and the places I visited, but I feel heavy with this new thing between us. There isn't much inflection in her voice and I can tell she's thinking about our kiss, too.

"Dublin Castle is nice, but you need to see a real castle. The kind you envisioned before you got here," she says. I watch her lips while she talks, remembering them on mine just a few short minutes ago. The intensity of the desire to kiss her again surprises me. Kerry is everything I don't want. She's stubborn, extremely opinionated, yet also sexy, determined, and smart. I sneak a quick sideways glance at her. I can't read anything on her face. I have no idea if that kiss meant anything to her. I turn my attention back in front of me, but it's too late. I smash into the street light and bounce off of it, instantly applying pressure to my forehead. It sounds like Kerry is laughing, but it's hard to hear over the bell ringing in my ears. Shit, that hurt. "This is why I'm taking you home." She hooks her arm around my elbow and keeps me close. "We might never see you again if I don't." I don't argue with her and keep my eyes forward. We walk for what feels like miles, but only is about five blocks.

"You know, I could have just walked back to Howth. It might have been faster," I say, pointing in the other direction. Kerry's laughter is low and raspy.

"We're almost to my house. You don't walk a lot of places back home, do you?" I don't even have to answer that because she already knows. We stop in front of a house that looks like a brownstone. It's sandwiched between two other houses with just enough space for a driveway. We head down the dark alley and instinctively I move closer to Kerry. She surprises me by putting her arm around my shoulders. She thinks I'm cold. I sigh at her warmth and snuggle against her. I love the smell of her. She smells like warm cinnamon and vanilla mixed with something spicy, like sandalwood. I lean in closer so that now we are walking like a couple. "Good news. There's no traffic this time of night to Howth, so we'll get there in no time." Most of the drive is in silence. Kerry flips on the radio so we are able to talk about music for about five minutes. I'm too tired to ask her what she's thinking. I lean back in the seat and relax. "Grace. Grace, wake up. We're here." I feel soft fingertips on my cheek, stroking softly up and down. I snuggle down deeper and sigh. "Grace. You need to wake up. Doesn't a warm bed sound much better than this cold car?" I crack open my eyes and look around. Kerry is leaning over me and smiling. For a split second, I almost reach up to touch her face, but I stop myself just in time.

"Okay." I turn over and face the other way in the seat.

"No, no. Get up. Come on. I'll help you up to the apartment. Abram misses you."

I sit up, finally waking up. Abram? "Where am I?"

"We are at the shop. Come on. I'll help you upstairs. Let's make sure you have heat up there." I slip my hand into her outstretched one and she gently, but firmly, pulls me up. I'm wobbly on my feet, so she holds me for a brief moment until

I'm steady. I stop myself from slipping my arms into her coat and hugging her waist. By the time we reach the apartment, I'm balanced, but tired. That whiskey kicked my ass. Thankfully, I don't talk a lot when I've been drinking or else I would have already made a fool of myself.

"Thanks for taking care of me tonight," I say. She unlocks the door and opens it for me to enter. She follows me. I stop and turn toward her. She averts her gaze.

"I'm going to make sure the heat is on before I leave you and this little guy." She reaches down to Abram who is desperate for attention. She breezes past me and disappears for a moment. I remove my jacket and throw it on the chair, but miss it by a mile. At least it's in the same room. I kick my boots somewhere near the chair. "Okay, the heat is on so you should be fine for the night." She heads for the door. I want to stop her, but I'm too confused so I watch her open the door and slip through. Before she closes it, she turns to me. "I'll see you in the morning."

"You were right. Thanks for taking care of me," I say. She winks at me and softly shuts the door.

Chapter Eight

The sun is bright and I hear and feel the steady hum of Abram next to me on the couch. I crack open my eyes and blink several times before I start moving around. I never made it to the bed. I'm stuck between the functional, yet not comfortable couch cushions, and a pile of purring fur. The clock strikes eight. I can't imagine Kerry is going to want to spend the day with me after last night. I was not planning on seeing her yesterday. I was not planning on kissing her. Actually, something in my brain tells me that she initiated it. I remember leaving the bar and I remember she followed me. I must have told her about my deal with Morgan because she kissed me. Oh, and it wasn't just a tiny kiss. It was a throw your body into it kind of kiss with heat, passion, and tingles. It was a really good first kiss. I need to get up and shower because I'm sure I smell like whiskey and cat. My wardrobe is seriously lacking. I have the jeans I wore on the way over to Ireland and I can wear a button-down shirt. Today is supposed to be warm. I take a much needed shower and hurry up at the speed of hangover to get ready in an hour. I need food. And a nap. I already want to go back to bed. But the idea of spending a day with Kerry motivates me to keep moving.

"Are you awake and dressed?" I hear from the living room.

"What is that?" I say. I was going to tell her good morning, but she is carrying a helmet and I'm pretty sure she's not wearing it to drive her car, even with me as a passenger.

"You need to have an open mind, Grace. This is the best way to see Ireland," she says. "It's a gorgeous day and I promise it won't be disappointing."

"Those things are dangerous! There is no way I'm getting on one." I stop shaking my head because it's only making my headache worse. "They aren't safe, Kerry."

"I haven't crashed yet. Well, only once in my car," she says, lifting her eyebrow at me. I take a moment to appreciate her outfit. She is wearing tight black pants, a form fitting cream sweater, and her leather jacket. Her hair is clipped back at the base of her neck, her creamy white skin exposed and perfect for kissing.

"I really don't think I can do this." I turn, but she reaches out and gently grabs my arm.

"Trust me, Grace. I won't hurt you," she says. "Let's go grab breakfast, just down the street, and if you don't like it, I will go get my car." She sounds so sincere.

"Okay, but just down the street," I say. She smiles that beautiful smile at me and I can't help but smile back. She hands me my jacket after I slip into my boots and follows me out of the shop. "What kind of motorcycle is this?" Not that I'm going to know if it really is good because the only motorcycles I know back home are Harley-Davidsons.

"A BMW F650GS, a popular and very affordable bike in Ireland. All of Europe actually. She's about ten years old, but still rides like a dream. Here, let me show you." She swings her leg over the seat and points to the helmet I'm clutching. "Put that on and let's go for a spin. Now, have you ever been on a motorcycle before?"

"I drove a little dirt bike for a summer when I was in middle school," I say. She explains where everything is on the bike. Not much has changed from when I learned years ago.

"Okay, hop on. Make sure your helmet is tight," she says. I feel stupid wearing it, but put it on anyway.

"How come I have to wear the full helmet, but you get the cool one?" I cinch the strap tight and flip down the plastic guard.

"Because I don't want anything to happen to your pretty face," she says. I smile. She said I was pretty.

"But nothing's going to happen, right?" I ask. She nods behind her indicating I need to saddle up. She slides forward making room for me on the seat. I take a deep breath and get on. Every part of my body is up against Kerry. Maybe this won't be so bad.

"Put your arms around my waist to hold on. When I lean, you lean," she says.

"Why would we be leaning?"

"Just hold on," she says. She starts up the bike, prompting me to hold her tighter. I clutch her side when the bike jolts forward into traffic. She reaches down and pulls my arm from around her waist and makes me link my hands together. My thighs are up against hers, spread wide. Thirty seconds on a motorcycle and I'm already turned on. I now understand this infatuation with bikes. I'm actually sad when, after a two minute ride, we are already at the café for breakfast. Kerry parks and taps my leg for me to get off. She leans forward so that I can slip off.

"That was fantastic!" I watch her remove her helmet and undo her hair clip. Her wavy hair, gorgeous and bright in the full sun, falls around her shoulders. Why do I always want to kiss her? A week ago, I didn't even like her.

"I told you. And since the day is warming up nicely, it will be perfect for a nice ride though the country. Come on. Let's get some food," she says. I watch as she swings her long leg behind her, the black pants hugging her every curve. I hand her my helmet when she turns to me, and she secures it to the bike.

"I didn't even feel the wind," I say.

She laughs. "That's because I was blocking it for you." She holds the door open for me and I enter the already busy café.

"Kerry, over here." A waitress waves to an empty table for two up against the back wall. I feel the warmth of Kerry's fingers press against my lower back, guiding me to the back of the café. We sit down and order coffee. I'm nervous. I'm not good at pretending the kiss last night didn't happen. I play with my coffee cup, twisting it in my hands, enjoying its heat. Kerry's accent is more relaxed, but I find that she's still easy to understand. I must be getting used to her voice.

"Since you aren't that familiar with riding yet, we won't go far today. I was thinking we should head up to Howth Castle and then to Wicklow. There is plenty to do in a day there and the drive won't be so bad," she says. She is very engaging and delightful with the waitress, not flirting, but just being nice. It's refreshing. I realize just how superficial I am back in Dallas and how my friends and I easily dismiss people who aren't in our social circle. I've been here in Ireland less than ten days, and I believe that this tiny country has already changed me. For several days, I haven't cared about work or my accounts. I've only cared about the people I've met.

"Tell me what your favorite thing about Ireland is," I say. She looks surprised at the question.

"I don't know if I can narrow it down to just one favorite thing. This is my home. My family has been here for generations. Ireland is a beautiful place to live. I'm in the city, but surrounded by country. I have the best of both worlds. It's not a big country, and certainly isn't one to accept change quickly, but it's my heart." She's so sincere and I believe this might be the answer that everybody gives me if I take the time to ask.

"From what I know and have seen since I've been here, I believe you," I say. She smiles. I want to ask her about last night, but she doesn't seem to be in a hurry to talk about it. I'm trying hard not to stare at her lips, or remember how they tasted and felt against mine, but it's hard to pretend that kiss isn't between us. And now that my body has been flush up against her, it's hard not to want to know. I cave.

"So why didn't you tell me about yourself after I shared my aunt's letter with you?" I ask. It's better than just blurting out the obvious question.

"I didn't think it was important," she says. Her indifference confuses me. Does she make it a habit to randomly kiss women? I know there's a history with Donna and her answers last night were borderline rude, but I can't imagine she can kiss somebody like that and not care a little bit. I decide to let it go. I can't be that clingy after one kiss.

"What is it like being a lesbian in Ireland?" I ask. "Was it hard to come out to your family? Did they care?"

"Maybe not as dramatic as yours because I almost always had girlfriends. It was not a surprise to my parents or my brother. Although he did tease me and tell me to stay away from his dates," she says.

"It wasn't great for me. My mom was sort of okay with it, but my dad still has a problem. We don't talk about it. I show up for Sunday dinners on occasion and we talk sports or current affairs." I don't have a lot in common with my father and that makes me miss my mom even more.

"Texas is big into sports, right?"

"You wouldn't believe it if I told you. Football is huge where I live. The high schools have giant college size stadiums because it's so popular. And by football, I don't mean soccer," I say. She smiles at me.

"I know. Although football, or soccer as you call it, is growing for you in America, right?"

I really don't want to talk about sports. I do enough of that with my dad. I nod. "Did you play sports in school?" I veer the conversation back to her.

"In secondary school, I played golf and some football," she says. "What about you?"

"I'm entirely too awkward to play any sports, but I do enjoy watching them. Except for soccer and golf. Those are the worst sports to watch ever."

Kerry laughs. "Duly noted. I would have played more, but Donna from last night, remember her? Well, she was on the

football team with me and we battled for the same girl a few
times. It just got to be too much so I quit the team and joined the
golf team instead. I missed my teammates, but for some reason
Donna had it out for me." She purses her lips and shrugs at me.

"Maybe she really liked you, but you somehow rejected
her. Usually that's the case," I say. "The straight girls fight over
guys, and the lesbians fight over one another. Maybe something
happened there. She seemed pretty nice." Kerry laughs.

"Yeah, well, it's okay to still harbor a grudge. I'm Irish after
all," she says.

"And a redhead, too," I say. We still aren't talking about the
kiss. I guess I'm just going to have to learn to let it go. The food
arrives and we dig in. I'm very hungry since last night's dinner
was whiskey and a few pieces of toast.

"Do you always drink like last night?"

"No, I rarely drink at all. That was the problem. I gave my
inexperienced self permission to drink since I am obviously not
driving while over here. I wish someone would have told me
that whiskey sneaks up on you. That would have saved me a ton
embarrassing decisions last night." I groan into my hands.

"Was asking me to kiss you embarrassing?" she asks.

"I didn't ask you to kiss me," I say, completely flustered by
her accusation. "I said that Morgan told me I needed to at least
kiss an Irish girl before I left. I didn't say it had to be you." I
can feel the heat in my cheeks, and my heart thrash in my chest.
I don't like confrontations, even if they are over something as
simple, yet life changing as a first kiss.

"I'm teasing you, Grace. I wanted to kiss you." I stare at her,
wondering how she can talk about this so calmly. I can barely
maintain eye contact with her.

"Oh," I look down at my plate, suddenly very interested in
my leftovers. What a weird and strangely exciting time with Kerry
I've had. I've gone from fearing her in a bad way after causing
her to wreck her car, to fearing her in a good way because of a

passionate kiss. I'm leaving soon. I need to rein this craziness in. I'm not in it for an affair or a long term relationship. I should have never allowed that seed of needing to kiss a girl over here to poke around in my brain. Now I'm in a tough spot. Maybe nothing happens now and we just have fun the next few days. I basically have zero plans until I leave except sell the car and figure out what to do with Abram. Leigh has agreed to take him, but I don't feel like it's the perfect fit. Apparently, she has a giant dog and I don't know how Abram will do with it. Funny how I'm already attached to that fur ball.

"So, what are we going to do now? I mean, what do you have planned for me next?" No matter how I say it, it sounds sexual to me. I'm slightly flustered, but she saves me.

"Well, we will get back on that bike and go see a castle. A real one with hundreds of years of history where lords and ladies lived and danced the night away," she says.

"Why, Kerry Mulligan, who knew you had it in you to be romantic?" I say, playing along with her.

"I'm full of surprises. Let's get out of here," she says. We hop on the bike, anxious to get our day started. I feel so much better now that I've had food and a ton of water. And, now that I know she wanted to kiss me, this day just got a whole lot more interesting.

CHAPTER NINE

Are you serious? I've been this close to a real castle and didn't even know it?" Our first castle is in Howth. It is exactly what I expected, only better. I wait for Kerry to unlatch her bag and hand me my camera. I can't wait to snap away.

"Didn't you do any research before you came here?" she asks. I shake my head. Morgan did most of the planning. I do remember something about a castle, but I just assumed it was as clean and new as Dublin's Castle.

"Tell me about this place." I lead the way even though I'm not sure where to go first.

"Well, I've scheduled a tour for us that will start in a few minutes. The guide will do a much better job of telling us its history. Go take some photos and I will find him." She doesn't have to tell me twice. By the time she finds me, I've already taken over one hundred shots. "Grace, this is Mac. He's going to give us a private tour of the place." I introduce myself to him and our tour is underway. It's well preserved and Mac is very thorough about the details. Kerry walks patiently beside me, adding a few words here and there. By the time it is over, I find out that it's over seven hundred years old, it's not the original castle, and the private owners don't like it if you run off to take photos.

"That was great. How did you manage to get us a private tour?"

"Ah, Mac owes me a favor. I found the perfect house for his daughter," she says.

"Well, thank you. It was fantastic," I say.

"We will hit another castle by the end of the day where you'll have free reign and can go anywhere inside and out to take photos. This is the closest," she says. She hands me my helmet and we head out, the Irish Sea on my left and the beautiful countryside on my right. I'm more comfortable holding her now that I know she wanted to kiss me. After driving for an hour and tapping her twice on her shoulder so that she could pull over for me to take photos, she finds a thin ropelike dirt trail and heads up it. The slope is pretty steep. Her body slips back into me and I spread my legs farther apart to accommodate her. Between her warm body resting against all of my sweet spots and the vibration of the bike between my legs, I am so ready for an orgasm. We plateau off and Kerry stops the bike.

"How about a quick lunch up here?" She slides off and grabs my hand to help me off the bike. I don't say a word when she continues to hold my hand and brings me closer to the edge of the cliff. "This is one of my favorite thinking places."

"It's spectacular up here. Very inspiring. I would be up here all of the time," I say, soaking in the beauty. She softly drops my hand and heads back to the bike. I miss the warmth of her hand already. I'm so confused, but so afraid that if I say something, this tenderness will disappear.

"My mother gave me a small loaf of bread and some cheese to nibble on during our outing today. I'm afraid I only have sparkling water to drink. We are almost to Wicklow so we can stock up on drinks there." She takes off her leather jacket and puts it on the grass. "We can sit on our jackets and watch the sea." I slide mine off, thankful that the day is warming up nicely. It's breezy, but not annoyingly so. "So you are either getting used to my accent even though we both know I don't have one, but you do, or you understand only about half of what I say." She tears off a piece of the bread and hands me the sliced cheese that has been in the tiny cooler with the cans of sparkling water. I laugh at her joke.

"I think I'm more relaxed now and I'm not worried about trying to understand everything all the time."

"I agree. You aren't as uptight as you used to be." She winks at me when I shoot her my mean, squinty eye look.

"When I first met you, I had only been in Ireland less than a day. I was completely frazzled and upset. What a horrible day that was," I say.

"I was an ass. Nobody got hurt. It's was actually quite funny," she says, smiling at me. "You had this look of pure horror on your face."

"You had this look like you were going to kill me and with good reason. I still can't believe I did that." She leans over and tilts my chin up to her. The relaxed version of Kerry is downright beautiful. Her dark green eyes sparkle in the sunlight and her red hair glows. I have a habit of reaching out and touching beautiful things. I refrain even though the desire to touch her is great.

"Don't worry about it. It's over and done." She leans forward and right when I think she is going to kiss me, she pulls back slowly. "Like I said, it was wrong of me to blame you for something that is out of your control."

"I've already decided to offer Leigh, Emma, and Conor some sort of severance package. My aunt would want me to take care of them somehow." I struggle to stay focused on our conversation.

"That's very generous of you," she says. I shrug. I don't know what's an acceptable amount that isn't insulting or too much. I need to concentrate on getting the place sold and not spend the money before I even get it. I will worry about actual amounts after the fact. "Okay, let's talk about something different. Tell me about your most recent relationship."

"Ugh. It was awful. I caught her in my bed with another woman."

Kerry winces. "Ouch. That's never a good thing."

"No. She used me and one day I decided to go home early to surprise her and she surprised me instead. It's so cliché. All the signs were there and I just ignored them, thinking she would be faithful to me no matter what. We were together for three years. I was supporting her while she finished her master's degree."

"What was she like? Obviously, you loved her so she had to have some good qualities," she says.

"The usual stuff. Charismatic, beautiful, and smart. Then we got comfortable and she didn't like my long hours and wanted somebody there for her. I was too wrapped up in work to care. I'm to blame for it, too."

"I've noticed that you are very much into your job. How many hours do you work a week? Like sixty or seventy, right? Think about how much you miss. I need at least one day to not think about work or houses or anything. It's hard to do, but I'm afraid that I will miss so much. Especially with Emma ready to give birth any day now. How am I going to be able to concentrate when the first baby in our family is here?" That makes me smile. She doesn't strike me as a baby person, but then again, I've had her pegged wrong since the beginning.

"That's definitely one thing I've noticed being over here. Everyone is very family oriented. Not that we don't have that back home, but I live in such a large community, that it's hard to connect with them. Honestly, I can't remember the last time I had a conversation with my neighbor." I frown at that realization.

"Most days I have to avoid my neighbors because if I don't, I will stand there talking to them for days," she says. I roll my eyes at her. "No, really. Mrs. Murphy is our ninety-year-old next door neighbor. She has nothing to do all day but try to catch us in the alley and talk. It is not unusual for one of us to be trapped for thirty minutes or longer." I like the way she says thirty. It sounds like 'dirty' and makes me smile. "I know you think I'm crazy, but it's true. When you meet my family, they will tell you that I only speak the truth." I've already met a lot of her family, all under crappy circumstances.

"How often do you come up here? It's beautiful," I say, looking out at the sea.

"I only come up here when I need to get away for a bit," she says.

"It's a wonderful view and you have all of these beautiful flowers ready to bloom. I bet in summer it's gorgeous." I reach down and pluck a tiny blue flower. "Leigh told me this is a forget-me-not. She said Ireland has plenty of different versions of this. I think it's beautiful that wildflowers are used in the bouquets. It adds so much character." I pluck a few just to have them as a token of my first and probably last motorcycle ride in Ireland.

"If you are done eating, let's head to Wicklow. I have the most amazing thing to show you." She stands up and reaches for my hand. I oblige and she pulls me up with little effort. For such a slender woman, she is very strong. I'm flush up against her and I think she is going to kiss me, but she releases my hand and picks up our jackets. I press the flowers into my napkin and safely tuck them inside my jacket pocket.

"I'm ready," I say, although I am reluctant to leave such a beautiful place. "How did you find this little piece of heaven?"

"One day I was riding around and saw this tiny dirt road and thought I would try it out. I've been coming here for years and have yet to meet a single person. I'm sure it's somebody's land, but they don't seem to mind or don't know that I come up here." She straddles the bike and slides up for me to climb on. Thank you, yoga, for insisting I stay in shape. I slip on behind her and take a moment to gather myself before I touch her waist. She turns to me. "The trip down might be tricky so hang on to me." Now I have permission to press up against her. I slide up, my thighs pressed against her. I'm trying not to think about my clit pressed up against her, too, but it's hard when the familiar throb appears, mimicking my heartbeat. I feel it speed up. She tightens my arms around her waist and moves forward. It takes us a few minutes of bouncing around before we hit the asphalt again. I'm ready to come. I'm seriously thinking of getting a motorcycle when I get home. I give her a thumbs up and loosen my hold on her waist. I lower my hands to her hips and hold them instead. I think she makes a noise, but I'm not sure.

We reach the quaint town of Wicklow in twenty minutes. I trust Kerry, my hesitation about being on the back of a bike gone. I'm having fun. She takes me to the entrance of a parkland where the biggest waterfall in Ireland is located. I'm so excited. There aren't a lot of people here because it's not summer and the food kiosks aren't open yet. I bypass the cute souvenir shop and head straight for the waterfall. It's magnificent. Since there has been a steady amount of rain, the waterfall is swollen, and thick, and the tiny sprays of water feel good in the warm sunlight.

"This should be your new get away place. It's perfect," I say.

"Too many people here most of the time. We got lucky today," she says. She is close to me again. I don't mind her nearness so much now. She reaches out and straightens the collar of my jacket. "I do believe Ireland agrees with you, Grace." She pulls me slowly into her, my heart speeding up, my mouth suddenly dry. I lick my bottom lip, drawing her eyes to my mouth. "You have a very sweet mouth," she says. I know she wants to kiss me, and I want her to, but I regretfully step out of her embrace.

"You know I'm leaving next weekend, right?" I ask. I'm torn between diving back into her and walking away. "We shouldn't start anything here." She nods her head in understanding, but the agreement doesn't quite reach her eyes. They are still bright and full of passion. She is making it hard for me to pull away.

"I know. This whole thing is crazy. I'm sorry." She pulls away and as much as I want to follow her and tell her it's okay, I know that I can't. Our relationship is balanced on a rocky start. The best thing for me is to go back home. I need to forget about the shop, not worry about the employees. I also need to get away from Kerry before I slip. It's not pretty when I'm needy. Plus she's thousands of miles from me. It's not as if I live on the east coast and can hop on a plane for a six hour nonstop flight for an extended weekend with her. I'm a total of fourteen hours from airport to airport, thanks to layovers and international-get-to-the-airport-two-hours-before-your-flight rules. Realistically, she doesn't want a relationship. She probably just wants a quick affair and then 'bon voyage' when I leave. I don't do quick and easy. At least I haven't yet.

"There are several castles in this gorgeous town. We can hit them and then do an early dinner. I promise to have you back to Howth before it gets dark." She's all tourist guide now, the passionate redhead no longer present. I'm saddened by the sudden loss of her heat. She doesn't hold my hand as we walk side by side on the path around the waterfall. I understand though. I can't have it all and I don't want to lead her on. I make it a point to keep the conversation lighthearted and ask boring questions instead of why? Why me? Why now? She went from cold to hot with me in an instant.

At least the castles keep my interest for a few hours and dinner conversation is relatively safe. I'm very intrigued about life in Ireland and ask a ton of questions about her life, her schooling, and what she does for fun. She goes out a lot with her friends, but only because she can't wait to get a place of her own. I can't imagine this cosmopolitan woman who knows a ton of people and hits the bars almost every night, is going to be happy raising sheep on a farm away from the city and the hustle of city life.

"So what are you going to do on your farm all by yourself?" I ask. I work at sounding sincere and not condescending. We haven't learned each other's tones yet.

"Hang out with the sheep and the chickens." She doesn't understand my question.

"I mean, what else are you going to do? It sounds like a lonely day all by yourself," I say. She smiles.

"Well, I'm sure my da won't let me off the hook so easily about walking away from the family business, so I will probably work part time for The Mulligan Group. And I don't plan on being alone forever," she says. I don't know if she's trying to make me jealous or not, but it works.

"I didn't figure you would be alone. You are too..." I stumble and catch myself from saying beautiful so I stutter out a nondescript word. "...fair." She busts out laughing.

"Fair? That doesn't even make any sense." I get caught up in her infectious laugh and chuckle, too.

"Okay, yeah, that was lame. I meant from what I know of you, you're a catch. You will make somebody happy. You know?"

"Well, it's too bad that you are leaving in what? Six days? Sad, actually." She doesn't elaborate and I don't push her.

"I might leave a little earlier." She jerks her head up and stares at me in surprise.

"Why? You should at least consider this a vacation and go do fun stuff," she says.

"It's not as much fun when I'm doing it alone." I don't give her a chance to offer because I'm afraid she will and then it will be impossible to keep my hands off of her if she is around me constantly. "It's too bad Morgan couldn't make it." Now why did I say that? I can tell I've hurt her feelings. "And I know you need to work," I quickly add. She gives me a non-committal half nod.

"So when would you leave?"

"Depends on what you need me for. I mean, what you need for me to do. Um, about the shop and anything that could come up." I can almost see her retreating into her professional self and I feel like an ass.

"Technically, we're done. I know that you want to sell the car, but we could make that part of the estate," she says, her voice void of the playful Kerry I've gotten to know so well the last couple days.

"I'm not ready to leave just yet. I mean maybe leave Wednesday or Thursday. That would give me the weekend home to recuperate. Jet lag and I do not get along." I try to add humor to our conversation, but it falls flat.

"We should probably get going if we're to get home before dark. I know you aren't entirely comfortable on the bike and besides, I made you a promise." She gets up and pays the ticket practically ignoring me until we get outside. I don't know what to say to her. I'm trying to protect myself, guard my heart because she is everything I'm attracted to, and completely out of my reach. I won't do long distance, not that she's asked. And I won't do a one night stand, not that she's asked that either. I have a feeling I will end up alone with twenty cats to keep me company in my old age. She hands me the helmet and slides forward to make room for me. This time I squeeze the seat with my knees for stability so that I don't have to clutch her and feel her against me. When we make it home, she stays on her bike and wishes me a good night. I touch her arm before she leaves, getting her attention for the first time in over an hour.

"Thank you, Kerry. Today was very special for me. Ireland is beautiful and you were right about the bike. It was a lot of fun," I say. She gives me a glimpse of a smile, like the one I saw on her face the day we met, and nods.

"Good night, Grace." I watch her disappear into the twilight, my heart heavy in my chest because I know I can't have her.

CHAPTER TEN

So, are you just going to stay in Ireland? You know, I wonder if we could open an office in Europe. You could be our International Creative Manager." It's so good to hear Morgan's voice.

"Ha. It is nice here, but I kind of miss the craziness of our world. Tell me what's going on. I'm going to check in with my crew next, but I wanted to hear what's really happening so that I can prepare myself. How's the pancake account? Are they happy with the ads? I haven't heard from Alisa since Friday." I've done a few things remotely, but I've mainly left all of my responsibilities to my second in charge, Alisa. She's competent and knows when to baby the accounts, and when to crack down. Funny how I'm forgetting about my job the longer I'm away from it.

"I think so. The changes were small. I'm sure they didn't want to bother you. We landed two more accounts last week that will need your love and attention, but that's about it." Morgan is great at swooping in and securing deals, but really bad at following up with them. That's where I come in. We talk about business until she's bored. "Tell me about Kerry. What's going on there?"

"We had a good day yesterday, but then I had to open my mouth and ruin it," I say.

"Oh, no. Did you do that clingy thing again?"

"Shut up, no. I did not. I actually kind of turned her down."

"No, you did not! Isn't she really gorgeous with Ariel hair?" I laugh at her reference to Disney's *Little Mermaid.*

"Then come home tomorrow. Why are you waiting?" She has a good point. I just don't think I can leave Ireland yet. I feel unsettled and I need to find out why.

"Eh, I have a few things left to do like get rid of Aunt Nola's car. And I'm thinking of taking a trip to Blarney. Come on. Who wouldn't want the gift of gab?" I ask.

"You know the Irish urinate on the Blarney Stone, right?" she asks.

I hesitate in disbelief. "Really? No."

"Truly. I've read all about it. I marked it off of our Ireland list. The castle looks cool, but I really didn't want to put my lips on that." I mentally mark that off of my list, whether it's true or not. "I'm scheduled to see the Cliffs of Moher tomorrow. I just want to see a few more things before I head back." I know I'm stalling to hopefully hang out with Kerry one more time even though it's the start of the work week and I'm sure she's going to be very busy, especially since I gave her the photos and she can now list the shop.

"Okay, well, let me know when you get in and I'll pick you up. I'm proud of you, Gracie. You finally got away and are doing something fun and for you." We say our good-byes and I spend the rest of the day reading work e-mails, reviewing products, and answering questions asked by my staff on ongoing projects. I'm surprised when there is a knock on the door.

"Grace? I'm shutting down the shop now. Would you like to join me and my husband for supper this evening? It won't be anything fancy." My stomach rumbles when I hear the word supper.

"I would love supper. I haven't eaten since breakfast." I jump up and spend a few minutes primping. My slacks and blouse aren't too wrinkled so I don't worry about changing. Today isn't as warm as yesterday, so I throw on a sweater and my jacket since we will be walking to Leigh's house.

"I'm glad Emma took the day off. She's going to have that baby any day now. She must be miserable," I say, making conversation as we trek up the hill.

"I agree. I thought it would be today since she is so uncomfortable," she says.

"Do you have any children?" I ask.

"None of my own, but my husband has two sons from a previous marriage. I helped raised them. Both boys are in the military, like their father was. I'm surprised you don't have any children. A beautiful young woman like yourself should have children."

"Thank you. I'm sure I will at some point," I say. "I'm in no rush."

"You work too hard." She reminds me of my mother who tells me that over and over.

"I haven't the last week and a half," I say.

"You are still working, just in a different capacity. Tell me your plans before you leave."

"I'm booked for a bus tour to see the Cliff of Moher tomorrow. Wednesday I need to clean out Aunt Nola's car and get rid of it. Right now, I'm flying out on Saturday, but I might change my flight since Kerry was able to get all of the paperwork done so quickly. I'm thinking of flying out Thursday. That will give me time to relax and adjust to Texas time before I start work again Monday."

"Well, it seems as if your trip so far has been nice. Kerry said she was taking you out yesterday. How was that?"

"She showed up on a motorcycle. At first I wasn't going to get on it, but as soon as I did and she took off, I was completely at ease. We went to Wicklow and saw the giant waterfall there. It was a good time." I don't want to tell Leigh about Kerry's special place because that's private.

"Kerry's a special lady. She has plans and is one of the hardest working people I know. Until I met you." I laugh. Leigh doesn't.

"Leigh, do you need a car? I'm more than happy to give you my aunt's. That way you can drive to work instead of walking."

"Thank you, Grace, but why don't you give it to Emma or Conor? They need it more than I do. Charles always drives places. It's not something I'm comfortable doing."

"That's a good idea. Since Emma's family is growing, I'll see if she wants it."

"Perfect. With the bar and a new baby, that family has a lot going on. And the tiny car Keagan has is not designed for a car seat. Conor has a motorcycle and I can't imagine he would want to give that up anytime soon." We are at Leigh's house in less than ten minutes, the walk not bad at all. We are greeted by a large dog and a burly man. I smile at Leigh's blush when Charles kisses her.

"Hello, Grace. Welcome to our home. Don't worry about Danga, he won't hurt you." Yeah, easy for him to say. The dog and I probably weigh the same. I'm sure his teeth are sharper than mine though. Danga is well behaved and sits down, waiting for me to pet him. A little bit of drool hangs from the corner of his jowls so I gently tap his head instead, purposely avoiding dog slobber. He seems fine with that and goes to sleep by the fire.

"Thank you for your hospitality. You have a wonderful and inviting home," I say. Both of them beam at me. Leigh ushers me into the living room and tells Charles to keep me company while she prepares supper. Charles has a very strong brogue so I really have to concentrate to understand him.

"So where are you from in America?"

"Dallas, Texas. I have a condo there." At his confused look, I elaborate. "An apartment that I own. I've lived there for about eight years."

"Leigh says you work a lot. What do you do?" He's genuinely interested in me so I take the time to explain what I do. He is very inquisitive and asks a lot of questions about advertising, especially television commercials. "Have you met a lot of famous people who work in commercials?"

"Most of our actors and actresses are just starting out and need a job or aren't too ambitious and just want a job for extra spending money. Although we have landed a few models who are pretty well known in the fashion industry." He smiles. I pull up our website and show him a few of the commercials we have posted.

"This is very good work. You should be very proud."

"Thank you. It's a job I really enjoy. I worked hard to get to this position."

"Okay you two. Supper is ready." I love how I'm already so comfortable in this home. We follow Leigh into the dining room. I'm surprised Danga hasn't moved. The smells in this house are divine and I can't wait to dig into whatever Leigh cooked.

"I started this stew yesterday. I hope you like mutton, dear," she says proudly. Lamb isn't my favorite, but it smells so wonderful that I graciously accept the large serving Leigh hands me. Charles passes around the bread. Before we start eating, they bow their heads for a dinner blessing. It's Gaelic so I don't understand it. Charles translates it for me.

"It means may you be blessed with a long life and good health."

"I'll drink to that," I say. I toast both of them and drink the wine. It's not a fancy wine, but a local one. Their daughter-in-law works at the winery and gifts them wine for any and every occasion.

"We don't drink a lot of wine so come over whenever you can so we have an excuse to open another bottle," Charles says. I find their conversation charming and I'm surprised when the clock strikes nine.

"I can't believe it's already nine," I say. "I've had such a good night with you that I lost track of time. I probably should go and let you have some of your evening to yourselves."

"I need to take Danga for a walk. Why don't you let me walk you back," Charles says. I offer to help Leigh clean, but she politely dismisses me.

"I will see you later, Grace. Thank you for being our guest." I give her a quick hug and head out with Charles and Danga.

❖

The bus leaves Dublin at eight in the morning so I catch the DART at six thirty to give myself enough time to find where I need to go. I know this will be a fun day trip for me, but I'm sad because I'm doing it alone. It's good for my self-esteem to get out and entertain myself. It's hard not to think of Kerry though since most of the fun stuff I've done has been with her. Our relationship is just confusing. I wonder if I will stay in contact with her after the shop sells. Maybe a few e-mails and only for a short time because I'm not convinced we really have much of a relationship. The tour bus is only a few blocks away from the train stop so I loiter for a bit. I make friends with a couple from Ohio who are also going on the tour.

"This is our fourth time to Ireland. I'm trying to convince Bob to retire here someday," Michelle says, nudging her husband with her elbow. "We usually stay on this side of it, but I told him that we needed to check out the entire island if we plan on moving here."

"Ireland is certainly different than back home. I find it refreshing," I say.

"I'm sure the weather here is so much different than down in Texas," Bob says. "We get the four seasons in Cleveland so we are used to it."

"Thankfully, I packed accordingly. It hasn't been too cold." Funny how even in a different country, we still want to talk about the weather.

The trip is long and totally worth it. I'm so glad everybody suggested taking the tour bus. There is just so much beauty throughout the land and I can't take enough pictures. By the time we reach the cliffs, I'm exhausted. I set out on my own to hike for a bit and set up a private picnic for one far enough away from the rest of the tourists. I'm in complete awe. I know love brought my aunt to Ireland, but it must have been the beauty and inspiration of this country that made her stay.

I fall asleep for the last two hours on the way back to Dublin. I wake up to a buzzing on my phone. Kerry texts me that she loved the photos and the listing is now live. I thank her and ask about her day. The desire to stay connected to her is strong now that I'm really not needed anymore.

Let's have supper tomorrow night. To celebrate.

Her invitation gets my heart racing. I play it cool and wait thirty seconds before responding.

Okay. Sounds good.

I will phone you tomorrow then. Sleep well.

You, too.

My second wind hits right as my head sinks into the feather pillow. I toss and turn for a bit, then decide to get up and get some work done. I check my e-mail and I download all of my pictures from today. My direct boss, Sherry, has asked me to take the lead on an account we've been trying to land for months. She has asked that I get back by Saturday so that I can relax before the dinner with our new potential client on Sunday night. Holy crap! I don't know if I'm ready to leave that soon. I check for flights out Thursday and Friday and find a red-eye Friday morning. That gives me tomorrow and Thursday only to say my good-byes. My first thought is Kerry. Not that there is anything there, but I was kind of hoping for a little bit more time just in case. Logically, I know that's stupid. Trying to start something with only a few days left is not smart. I'm not that kind of girl. I was the one who stopped her from kissing me in Wicklow. I can't even make up my own mind about her. I sigh and send my boss an e-mail that I have changed my flight and will be back on Friday so that I will be well rested in time for the meeting. I check in with Alisa, answer a few questions from one of the teams, and send my brother a quick e-mail. I gloss over the details and downplay the inheritance. I don't need that grief. It's two in the morning and the only thing left for me to do is sleep, something that still doesn't come easy.

CHAPTER ELEVEN

I take extra care for my date with Kerry. It's not a date, I tell myself as I carefully apply just the right amount of makeup and twirl one last time in the mirror. I'm wearing slacks and a blouse, the nicest things I brought with me. My jacket is a bit casual for the outfit, but I know the nights get cold so I'm stuck with it. I open the door and am greeted with a low whistle.

"Well, look at you. All cleaned up and looking very nice," she says. I blush.

"Thank you. I wasn't sure where we're going and you've seen me almost exclusively in jeans and boots."

"You look great. Are you ready?"

I nod and grab my purse. "Where are you taking me?"

"Hopefully, giving you a taste of Ireland that you won't forget," she says, her accent strong on purpose. I laugh and follow her out. I'm not sure if she's aware of her innuendo, but I certainly am.

"And here I thought you were picking me up on your motorcycle," I say. She opens the door for me and I slip into her recently repaired Volkswagen.

"I suppose I could go home and get it," she says.

"Don't you dare. I like being warm," I say. I put my hands in front of the vents, happy to feel the heat right away.

"Agreed. Do you want to know where we are going?" The twinkle in her eyes is adorable. I nod. "Nah, I'd better just wait and show you instead."

"You tease," I say. She winks at me. We head into light traffic and our conversation is smooth and easy. I honestly feel like I'm on a date. I'm nervous and exhilarated. My hands are sweaty and my mouth is dry. Yep, all the classic signs are here. This is a date. She surprises me by driving through Dublin and not stopping. "Are we leaving Dublin?" She smiles at me.

"Our dinner will be in a little town just south of here. Dun Laoghaire. But that's all I'm telling you," she says. I'm intrigued, even though we did drive through it on our trip down to Wicklow. She tells me some history about the town. I now have an excuse to look at her while she drives and talks to me. Her hair is loose and flows in waves over her shoulders. The gray cashmere sweater shows off her curves and I'm trying not to look at her body, but failing miserably. "So what do you think?" I look back up at her eyes.

"Umm. About what?" I ask, totally busted.

"Can you imagine waiting your whole life for your love to return to you only to find out he was murdered the day after he left your arms? It's one of the saddest stories I remember hearing when I was growing up." I have no idea what she is talking about because I was so busy looking at her, wishing I could be closer to her, that I completely missed the story.

"That's awful," I say, hoping that my response is appropriate.

"The poor woman had the opportunity to love time and time again, but turned away every honorable man because she was waiting."

"Oh, is that where the forget-me-not flower gets its name from?" I remember Leigh told me a story that seemed similar.

"No. The flower got its name from a knight who fell into the river and drowned. He was picking flowers for a woman he was courting and the weight of his armor caused him to flip over and drown. Before he died, he tossed the flowers at her and begged her not to forget him."

"What is with Ireland and the sad stories?" I ask. She laughs.

"That's not even an Irish story. And that's only one version of how the tiny flower got its name. There's one about God naming the flowers and skipped over the tiny blue flower and the flower spoke up. So God named it forget-me-not," she says.

"You should have gone to school to become a historian because you know so much folklore and history of Ireland. You missed your calling," I say.

"No. Everybody else already knows all of this. Since you're not from here, I can impress you with useless bits of information."

"So you are trying to impress me, huh?"

"Is it working?" she asks, a hopeful smile on her lips. I'm not sure why, but I flirt back even though I know it's a bad idea for both of us.

"Definitely," I say. I look away because her look is no longer playful, but rather intense. Enough to make me gulp and think about what it would be like to have just one night with her. One selfish, give everything, take everything night where neither one of us worries about the morning or the next week. She turns up a private road and once we round the corner, a beautiful, fully lit castle comes into view. I gasp. "Oh, my God. This is beautiful. Wait. We're having dinner here?"

"A private chef owes me a favor. You will love his food. He's fantastic," she says. She parks the car and I jump out, anxious to see it all at once.

"Kerry, this is too much! You should have saved your favor," I say, secretly excited that she used it on me.

"I wanted to celebrate tonight. The shop is officially up for sale and this is the perfect way to do it. Come on, let's take a look around," she says, grabbing my hand. I walk briskly beside her, trying hard not to skip with pure joy. What a perfectly romantic night. She takes me to the front of the castle where we are greeted by a gentleman dressed in a black suit who I assume is some kind of butler.

"Welcome to MacCabe Castle. Please follow me, ladies," he says. We fall in step behind him admiring the wall art and medieval decorations.

"This is incredible. You obviously are a good person to know here in Ireland. I got lucky," I say, instantly regretting my words when she raises her eyebrows at me. I have the decency to blush. The butler ushers us into a room with a giant stone fireplace and a small dinner table set up near it. I feel like I'm in a scene from *Beauty and the Beast*. I'm waiting for the tableware to jump into a song and dance routine. The butler informs us that the chef will be out momentarily. "Kerry, really, how did you manage this?" She smiles at me.

"I called in a few favors. Since you are leaving this weekend, I thought it might be nice to have a night…" she pauses, and corrects herself. "Have a meal you won't forget. And you are frowning because?"

"I'm actually leaving late tomorrow night. My boss called and wants me back in time to woo a client on Sunday. I'm not happy about it because I have a lot of loose ends here." She tries to wipe the surprise look off of her face, but it's too late.

"I'm disappointed, but I understand." She looks at me and forces a smile. "Then let's enjoy the food and conversation." I don't like that her guard is up again. Thankfully, the chef, an older gentleman with salt and pepper hair, enters the quaint dining hall and makes a beeline for Kerry, interrupting my depressing news.

"You look beautiful as always," he says, kissing both of her cheeks.

"Thank you, Ryan. You are always so kind. Please meet Grace Danner from America. She and I are working on a commercial project together." She's so politically correct.

"It's my pleasure," he says, nodding his head in my direction. "Ladies, let me go over tonight's menu." He pours us a glass of wine and discusses, in great detail, what he's going to cook this evening. Everything sounds delicious. When he leaves, Kerry lifts her wineglass in my direction.

"Here's to you, Grace. Thank you for making the trip here and working with me. I know I wasn't the easiest person when we first met, but hopefully you have a better opinion of me now." We are too far apart to clink glasses.

"And here's to you, Kerry, for getting the job done and showing me Ireland in a way nobody else could have. I loved the motorcycle ride and your private spot up on the cliff. I hope that our new friendship will continue even when I leave this beautiful place." We both take a drink and for a split second, she flashes me a look of hunger over the rim of her glass. It's so fast that I almost miss it, but my stomach starts quivering so I know I didn't imagine it. I manage to stifle my cough until I place my glass down.

"Are you okay?" she asks. I nod and hold up a finger to let her know I only need a moment. We shared a very passionate kiss this week and that look is the same look she gave me right before she kissed me.

"Sorry about that. Must have gone down the wrong pipe," I say. She lifts her eyebrow at me. How the hell am I going to get through this night? Everything is rushing at me: my departure tomorrow night, the undeniable passion we have for one another, and the angst of selling the shop and what that means to everybody involved. I'm too emotional right now.

"Dance with me while we wait for dinner. I'll show you how the Irish love not only whiskey and beautiful women, but we're all excellent dancers." She doesn't give me a chance to say no. Not that I would because watching her walk toward me, sexy and confident, is mesmerizing. She reaches for me and I do not hesitate. Her hand is warm in mine. When she pulls me toward her, my heart quickens and I lick my lips as my mouth moves very close to hers. I can feel her warm breath on my cheek and

I stifle another shiver. Pressed up against her strong, lean body, she effortlessly guides me around the room and over toward the fireplace. How she is still single is a mystery. She's beautiful, smart, and she makes me want to be a better person than I am. My body responds to her nearness. I can't get close enough to her. Every part of me is touching her and our bodies stop moving. Now she is simply holding me. My heart threatens to burst when her eyes meet mine and I feel her tighten her grip around my waist. I know that if she kisses me now, I will lose myself in her. She doesn't say anything to me, but stares at me, as if she's waiting for permission from me.

This beautiful, yet confusing moment is broken when Chef Ryan delivers the first round. I don't know if I should be grateful for his interruption, or hate him for it. I feel her hesitation to let me go as if this will be the last time our bodies are this close. I wonder what would have happened if Chef Ryan waited a minute or two before delivering our first course. Would we have kissed again? I try hard to focus on his explanation of the first course, but I can only look at Kerry. Her eyes never leave mine. I wonder if he knows he interrupted us. I wonder if he realizes he either stopped something incredible from happening, or saved us both from undeniable heartache. She breaks eye contact to respectfully pay attention. I take a deep breath and listen to him as well. After nodding and not understanding a word he just said, he places a tiny serving of baked oysters and sauce in front of me. I look up at him like he's crazy. I can eat this in one bite. He laughs.

"Don't worry. I promise you will be full by the end of the meal." I have the decency to blush. Kerry laughs at me, too. Chef Ryan leaves us again.

"I promised you a meal you wouldn't forget." She emphasizes the word meal, teasing me. My blush deepens. "Taste it. I want to see what you think." I nervously bring the fork up to my mouth knowing full well she is watching me, focusing on my lips and the quick flick of my tongue as I eat the oyster.

Watching her watching me is far more erotic than if she were to reach over and feed me herself. The desire in her eyes is unmistakable. She doesn't try to hide it and I don't look away. Her mouth opens slightly at the stifled moan I make. I'm sure if I were closer, I could hear her intake of breath, the hitch as her excitement grows.

"It's very good." I keep the conversation boring as I remind myself over and over that I'm leaving in twenty-four hours and not to flirt with her. Oh, what the hell. "No, it's perfect, Kerry. Thank you for bringing me to this incredible place. I'm anxious to see what else is on the menu." I reach for my glass. I don't miss the surprised look on her face that she quickly erases or the fact that she leans back in her chair to study me. She's wondering if I'm flirting, or if my actions are innocent. Historically horrible at seducing, I resort to the only thing I know how to do. I bite my lip, slowly, seemingly subconsciously, as I study the wine bottle. I notice she shifts in her chair a bit and leans forward. I have her attention. "So tell me about the people you've dated."

"Not much to tell really," she shrugs. "Girl meets girl, girl dates girl, girl decides girl isn't the one. Being single isn't horrible." This is true.

"How is that possible that you're single? Tell me what happened with your last girlfriend. Did your family get to know her? How did you meet?"

"Do you really want me to talk about another woman on this special night?" She smiles knowingly at me, her gaze intense, her body language rigid. "Do you want to know if I liked her? If I loved her? If the sex was fantastic? Do you want to know if I took her to my secret spot like I took you? Now, that is a question I can answer. No, Grace. I didn't. You are the only one who has been there with me." I can feel my cheeks redden with a mixture of desire and embarrassment.

"Why me then? Why take me there?" I ask. My stomach clenches with anticipation as I await her answer.

"Maybe because I know you're only visiting." Ouch. I wasn't expecting that.

"Not because you wanted to share it with me, but because I will keep your secret. How sad," I say. I pout at her and she smiles at me.

"Well, maybe another reason, too."

"Oh, yeah?" Now I'm intrigued.

"And because you are a special woman and I enjoy spending time with you. I truly will be sad when you leave." She pauses and I think she is going to say more, but we are interrupted by Chef Ryan who brings out the entrée.

"Ladies, roasted pork stuffed with potatoes and apples. Please enjoy," he says.

"This smells great. I have had nothing but fantastic food here in Ireland and have met the nicest people. I will miss everybody when I leave."

"Were you able to finish up everything with Nola's belongings?"

"The only thing pending is my aunt's car. I was thinking of giving it to Emma because she's going to need a car with a new baby. Do you think she would be receptive to that?"

"Grace, I could kiss you right now! That's extremely generous and I think after the initial shock, she would love it. A wonderful gift. Really." I'm focusing on the kissing part of what she just said. I think back to our kiss. It was fast, exciting, exhilarating, and left us both speechless. She might pretend that it didn't affect her, but I was right there and I felt every part of her against me. Her body was just as aroused as mine.

"It helps me out because I wouldn't know what to do with it otherwise. Leigh says she doesn't like to drive. Oh, and I would like to give Conor the delivery van. I know it's a basic model, but more reliable than what he has now. I'm sure he can just scrape off the decals."

"I'm speechless. Both will be extremely grateful. Conor can get rid of that awful scooter he calls a motorcycle and Emma won't have to take the train anymore. My brother is going to be so relieved. You have no idea how much that is going to help them." Her appreciation for her friends and family is remarkable.

"I'll sign the deed over tonight. Please tell her from me if I don't see her tomorrow at the shop. She's missed the last few days at work. I hope everything is fine," I say.

"She's been pretty miserable for sure," Kerry says. "I think the doctor is off on the delivery date. I can't imagine her lasting another week and a half."

"Leigh said the same thing. I can't believe she's still walking as much as she has been since I've been here." I already know I would be a complete mess who stays in bed every day whining about how miserable I am. Emma's my hero. She hasn't complained once about how swollen she is or how her back is killing her. "I would like to send some baby stuff from the United States. Not that you don't have super cute things here, but a variety might be nice. Do you think that would be okay? Or maybe a car seat?" I'm not up to speed on safety regulations here in Ireland about baby car seats, but I know the ones back home have survived some pretty horrific wrecks. I keep envisioning a handmade seat belt of fisherman's netting that Emma's dad has created for the baby. I cringe at my out of control imagination. The need to send a safe one to Emma and Keagan is suddenly great.

"The car is already too much, Grace. You certainly can do what you want, but it's truly not necessary."

"I wish I had more friends who had children. It's always so much fun buying cute little outfits and toys." I stop talking because I know I sound like I want to flash my cash some more.

"My da has made so many wooden toys already that the child won't get to play with for years. And only after the teething stage. The whole family is excited for the baby to arrive." Kerry looks down at her cell phone after a series of text messages light it up and jumps up, jarring the table. "Oh my! You aren't going to believe this, but they are taking Emma to the hospital right now. Her water broke."

Chapter Twelve

L et's go." I don't even hesitate. I grab a piece of bread and eat a few more bites as Kerry rushes to find Chef Ryan. She returns, grabs my hand, and we hurry back to the car.

"Ack. I don't even know what to do first," she says.

"I'd offer to drive, but I'm too freaked out," I say. She laughs.

"No, no. It's okay. Let me just take a moment." She takes a slow, deep breath and starts the car. "Let's go meet this new baby." Even though she is speeding, she is careful about it. The hospital is thirty minutes away in Dublin, but I'm sure we will make it there in twenty-five. She asks me to text Keagan and find out where they are in the hospital. I pick up her phone and get the information quickly.

"He says they just got there and for us to head to the maternity ward." I watch as she smiles at the news.

"We will probably be there in ten minutes." We are already in Dublin and since it's a weeknight, the streets are not congested. I hang on as she quickly maneuvers through the traffic, zipping in and around until I see the hospital up ahead. I'm feeding off of her anxiety so that by the time we find the information booth, I take over and start asking all the questions about where to find Emma and the rest of the family. The attendant directs us upstairs where we find the majority of the family hanging outside of the suite.

"Thank God you made it." An older woman grabs Kerry and clutches her. "Your brother is driving me crazy."

"What's going on? How's Emma?" Kerry gets answers from at least three different people all at once. I count twelve family members waiting outside. Her dad is quietly pacing near the door.

"We are waiting for the doctor to check her. Keagan is in there now. As soon as they let me, I will be in there, too." A lady who is unmistakably Emma's mother tells us. She is just as lovely as Emma.

"This is Grace Danner." Kerry introduces me to the group and names are thrown at me, names I won't remember in thirty seconds. I'm calm now and not worried about what they might think of me or if they've even heard about me. They have too much going on. I feel like I'm watching a play unfold right in front of me.

"Is everything settled with your aunt's estate? Has Kerry squared things away?" Kerry's dad is suddenly beside me. I nod. I'm sure he needs to talk about something else right now to keep from falling apart.

"The listing went up yesterday so I'm sure things will be happening soon," I say.

"It's a premium spot so I'm sure it will sell quickly," he says. Funny how that makes me sad now. "Kerry said you took the pictures. You did a good job."

"Thanks. It's what I do back home in the states. I work for an advertising agency and always jump in when photos need to be taken for projects."

"So you travel with all of your camera equipment everywhere?"

"Oh, no. Not all of it, but I have enough lenses with me for the just in case moments. And I didn't mean to take away any work from your photographer. I was just in the moment and I missed taking photos."

"You did a better job than Brian could have done. And don't worry about him. He's a contractor and not always reliable." That inflates my ego even more. We're interrupted by a disgruntled nurse who doesn't like that we are hanging out in the hall by Emma's room. She ushers us into a waiting room only twenty feet away.

"Now, I don't want to see any of you loitering outside of that girl's door. She's got enough on her mind," she says, eyeing us warily. "When the baby gets here, then you can take turns if, and only if, the doctor says so." Thankfully, we are the only ones in the small waiting room. Some of the family head out to smoke or get fresh air, while the rest get comfortable on the chairs and couches. This is going to be a long night.

"Did you find out what happened tonight with Emma?" I ask Kerry.

"She was home and in bed. She's been very uncomfortable the last few days so she was just resting. When she went downstairs to talk to Keagan who was working in the bar, her water broke and all hell broke loose. Everybody at the bar panicked, but Luce, one of the waitresses, who has had a few kids of her own, told Keagan to get the car. She called Da and told him they were headed to the hospital and they should head there as well. Apparently he or my mother called the entire family, hence the reunion here."

"Thankfully, she was here and not on the train or something. I can't even imagine if that were to happen," I say.

"Oh, I'm sure somebody would have gotten her to the hospital," Kerry says.

"Back home, somebody would have called the police and wouldn't have moved her at all to avoid a lawsuit," I say. She interrupts me.

"Why would there be a lawsuit?"

"Well, if something happened to her or the baby," I say, surprised she is surprised.

"Are you serious? That's crazy. I would want somebody to get me to a hospital any way they could. I wouldn't want my baby to be born in the back of a police car by somebody who couldn't deliver it right." She says. Her accent is stronger now that she's around her family and in a stressful situation. I nod in understanding only because I don't want to get into a conversation about what all could go wrong since her sister-in-law is about to give birth. This is their moment and I'm only here because Kerry is my ride tonight. I do like being a part of this big family, thrown into the midst of this incredible moment. I've never been a part of such organized chaos. There are several conversations going at once, but everybody is aware of one another. I see Kerry darting looks at her mom, while keeping the conversation going with her aunt. Her hand is resting against my leg so I know she is paying attention to me as well. Her mother, talking to her father, is aware of the door and of Luke who is pacing in front of it. I watch as she finally reaches out to calm him and draws him into their conversation. It's such a fantastic dynamic.

"So, technically, Grace is Emma's boss," I hear Kerry say to her aunt. That draws my attention back to them. I hadn't even thought of that.

"Not really. The shop seems more of a self-governing thing," I say. "Emma, Leigh, and Conor are all fantastic workers and just do what needs to be done."

"I'm sorry to hear about your aunt. I've only ever heard good things about her," Kerry's aunt says. We're interrupted by a very pale Keagan who bursts through the door, silencing everybody at once.

"Everything's fine so far. They just gave her the epidural so she's more comfortable," he says. His dad clamps his hand on Keagan's shoulder, his way of showing support. It's a surprisingly touching moment and tears spring to my eyes as I watch the love pass between this family. "She's ready for you," Keagan says, nodding at Emma's mom. She jumps up, straightens out her clothes and leaves the room with Keagan.

"Well, it shouldn't be much longer now," Kerry's mom says. Four hours later, everybody is quieter, a little more comfortable, but there is still a level of stress in the room. I'm leaning against Kerry and I don't even care who sees us. Nobody seems to mind though. I'm tired, still hungry and need to get up and stretch, but I like being this close to Kerry. She's warm, comforting, and it just feels right. I can't believe that I'm leaving in less than a day. We hear a yelp coming from down the hall and we all jump up.

"It's a boy! We have a baby boy!" Keagan yells all the way down the hall to us. The whole room erupts with laughter and tears of joy. Kerry pulls me into a giant hug and I can feel the stress of the situation leave her body as she relaxes into me.

"I have a nephew," she says. She leans down and kisses me soundly. We break apart breathless and smile. She leaves me to make her way to her brother who is in a giant hug with their parents. I cry when I see their emotional exchange. He takes Luke, his parents and Kerry down the hall so he can introduce them to Ian Brann Mulligan. The family celebration leaks out into the hall until a nurse tells us to either stay in the waiting room and keep our voices down, or go outside. Every single person goes outside and one of Kerry's uncles, Kent Mulligan, passes out cigars. I've never smoked one in my life, but it's so appropriate that I can't help but partake in this time old tradition. I grab a cigar, but before anybody lights theirs, Emma's mom finds us.

"If you want to hold the baby, you cannot smoke those," she says, before leaving. "That boy's first day on earth isn't going to be spent smelling smoke."

"Smoke them when you all get home later today," Kent says. One of the cousins breaks into a beautiful song and is quickly joined by others in the family. I don't know the song but it's sweet and they are killing it. I take out my phone and record it, knowing that Kerry will want to see this. I don't even think they notice I'm recording it. When it is done, there are more hugs, some whining about not being able to smoke the cigars, but mostly just a continuous celebration including impromptu dancing, bar type singing, and a fantastic celebration of new life. This kid is definitely going to be spoiled.

"Tell me they haven't corrupted you while I was away." Kerry is suddenly beside me, her warmth welcoming. I turn and slip into her arms and she holds me for a minute. I know this is an emotional night for the entire family.

"How's baby Ian?" I ask.

"Beautiful. A bundle of perfection. Would you like to meet him?" she asks.

"But there are so many people here who still want to see him. They should meet him first," I say.

"Look at them. They are singing, dancing, and aren't worried about getting in next. When did the Jameson come out?" she asks, referring to the flask someone is passing around.

"About the time Emma's mom said we couldn't smoke the cigars," I say. She laughs.

"I told you my family has tons of black sheep. I just didn't share that they are all here right now." She slips her hand in mine and we walk back into the hospital side by side.

"You know, I haven't held a lot of babies in my life," I say, suddenly very nervous.

"Just pretend he's Abram. You're pretty good with him," she says.

"I'm serious."

"You will be fine. I trust you." She squeezes my fingers. I still feel out of place when we peek into the room. Emma looks tired, but beautiful as always. Keagan is helping her sit up straighter in bed.

"Grace. I'm so glad you're here. Come and meet little Ian," Emma says.

"Congratulations. He's beautiful," I say. Kerry scoops him out of her father's arms and passes him to me. Good news, he's swaddled. Bad news, I hope I don't look as awkward as I feel trying to get him comfortable in my arms.

"He won't break," Keagan says.

"I told Kerry I'm not a great baby holder," I say. "I haven't held a baby since my cousin was born ten years ago." This probably isn't true. I finally get him tucked so we're both comfortable and I look at his gorgeous shock of red hair and tiny red fuzz where his eyebrows will be. He's every bit a Mulligan and I'm trying hard not to tear up again.

"See? You're doing fine," Emma says. I gently bounce him and walk around the room, no longer worried about others watching me. He tiredly opens his eyes at me, fighting hard to keep them open.

"He sees your blonde hair," Kerry says, her voice low. "I'm sure he's trying to figure out how to grab it."

"I'm sure his brain hasn't learned how to do that yet," I say. Her face is very close to mine and Ian's and I hold my breath when she leans down and nuzzles his cheek. It's a very loving move and I already know Kerry's wrapped around his little finger. "Well, that didn't take long."

"What do you mean?"

"You're already completely smitten by him," I say. She smiles at me and surprises me by kissing me softly.

"He's a Mulligan. What's not to love?" I gently hand him back to her, unnerved by my emotions. This woman is derailing me. The Kerry I met when I first got here was obnoxious, rude, and just pissed me off. The woman before me now is caring, generous, and sweet. She makes my head spin. This whole trip has been one life altering experience. I came here with the intention of selling a business, making a ton of money in the process, and returning to Dallas after a few fun days eating good food and drinking dark beer. Now, I'm dreading my flight out later today. I slipped and fell in love with Ireland and the people here. I need to leave soon and once I do, I should be fine. I will go back to my life of corporate America and shallow friendships. I will hang out with Morgan and we both will settle into relationships that are complacent and predictable.

Kerry holds baby Ian close to her chest, close to her heart. He nestles against her warmth, the trust between these two people immediate and true. I feel my own heart swell and threaten to burst at the love I witness. I wipe away the tears that are on my cheeks, their presence a reminder that I am vulnerable. Kerry kisses him good-bye and hands him back to Keagan.

"I'll send the others in one by one. We're going to take off. I need to get Grace back to the shop to get ready to fly back home," Kerry says.

"You are leaving already? I thought you were staying until the weekend," Emma says. I lean down and give her a hug.

"My boss asked me to come back sooner. It was such a pleasure to meet you. I'm so happy for your family and baby Ian," I say. Keagan even gives me a hug. I tell myself not to cry again, but I fail miserably.

"What an emotional night," I say, grasping at anything to say.

"Definitely. I know I will be exhausted. In about an hour, it will be light out. Come on, I want to watch the sunrise with you." Kerry and I head back to the car after sending some of the family up to the room. The rest are perfectly happy being unruly, singing, and dancing in the parking lot. Back home, they would have been arrested. Here, their celebration of new life is left alone. We spend most of the drive talking about Ian and first babies in the family. She pulls onto a dirt road and drives for a half of a mile, ruts and divots completely ignored. I wonder how often she needs to replace her shocks.

"The sunrise is gorgeous. Not as fantastic as the sunset, but I think this is a great way to leave Ireland."

"I'm pretty sure half of my guts are back there on this makeshift road," I say, pointing behind us.

"Yeah, I'm sorry about that. It's hard to see the road in the dark," she says. This is a road?

"So how do you know this place?"

"This is actually my uncle's property. He won't mind. He never comes here. I hate for it to go to waste." We finally park under a few trees. I get out and stretch, thankful that even though I got bounced around, I made it in one piece. Kerry hands me a flashlight. "I just need to get something out of the trunk." She grabs a large blanket and heads toward me. "Let's go." She offers no explanation, only her hand. I grab it and walk next to her in the dark, the shaft of light bobbing with every step I take.

"How far are we walking?" I ask. I'm bummed that I'm not wearing my comfortable boots.

"Not far, but you might have to climb a bit. I hope that's okay," she says.

"No worries. I'm a tough girl."

"Of course you are," she says. We hit our destination in only a few short minutes. Kerry fans out the thick, wool blanket and sits down, patting the spot beside her. "Have a seat. It gets cold just sitting here without it." I sit down and she wraps the corner around me so that we are both holding an end over our legs. I shiver a bit, excited to be alone with her again and so close. She's deliciously warm, and I'm trying hard not to scoot closer to her.

"Why do you have so many secret hiding places?"

"They aren't really hiding places, just places I love to be. Sometimes I need absolute quiet or just the ocean and having lived here my entire life, it would be a shame if I didn't have a private place to go." We are quiet for a bit, watching the sky lighten off in the distance.

"Thank you for everything you've shared with me, Kerry. Your time, your family, and your special places." I smile at her, my way of keeping it simple even though my stomach is quivering and my heart is galloping in my chest.

"Grace." That's all she says before she pulls me closer to her and kisses me. It's not a simple, sweet thanks for staying with me tonight kiss. This is an all-consuming, take my breath away kiss that makes me moan when she deepens it. She leans up and over me, never breaking the kiss, to settle between my legs. I forget about being cold. Her heat instantly warms me and even though I'm trying not to seem desperate, I can't help but pull her into me. I run my hands up and down her body, feeling the softness of her curves and the sharpness of her hips as they dig into me. I'm going to come before she even touches me if she continues to grind against my clit. I hold her firmly against me. I have never given myself to anybody so completely, so purely before. Maybe it's because I'm leaving today and I don't have to think about seeing her again, or maybe it's because I know I won't. She reaches over and pulls her half of the blanket over us. I don't even care that it's cold or that the ground is hard beneath us. I only feel her. She breaks the kiss to shed her jacket, then pulls me up by the lapels of mine to take mine off, too. Her energy is fierce and I'm taken aback by it. Her stare is intense and I shudder believing that I am the only person who matters to her at this moment, even if I'm not. This aggressive Kerry makes me whimper with need. I want her to touch me everywhere. I lift my hips up to greet her as she returns to me, my body greedy for friction. She takes the opportunity to slip a hand beneath me, her thumb only inches from my wet core. I reach down and pull her sweater up, excited to feel her skin for the first time. It's smoother than I imagine and I smile at the chill bumps that race against my touch.

"Are you cold?" I ask, leaning in for another kiss from her wet mouth.

"I'm on fire. It's your touch that is doing this to me," she says. I pull her down again and wrap the blanket around us anyway. She moves down to my neck, sucking hard enough to make me moan. I want to feel her teeth against my skin, scraping the tenderness raw. I selfishly press her head into me, telling her I want more. When her teeth dig into me, I buck into her, my hands grabbing her hips, holding her close. I hiss my approval as she continues to nip and suck all the way down to my cleavage. I release her hips and reach up to unbutton my blouse, slowing my movements when I feel her lips and tongue on my fingers. It's such an erotic feeling when she sucks my finger into her mouth, her tongue circling it slowly then rapidly. It's driving me crazy. I run my thumb over her bottom lip, dying to have the fullness inside my mouth again. She releases my finger and we instantly kiss, both of us needing that connection again. This time she helps me with my buttons, tugging the shirt out of my slacks, just as anxious to feel me as I am to feel her. I lean up so that I can take my shirt completely off at the same time she rips off her sweater. I take a moment to look at her in the budding light. Her skin is alabaster, a pale creaminess I've never seen or touched before. I run my fingertips from her sternum down to the top of her waistband. I unfasten her top button and slowly unzip them, never breaking eye contact. When I see her shiver, I assume she is cold and I pull her down. She grabs the corner of the blanket again and covers us, shifting so that she is more to my side than on top of me. I miss the comfort of her weight and turn to face her.

"I like you between my legs," I say. Her response is a very passionate kiss. I moan with delight as her hand slides down my stomach and over my slacks to touch my very wet, very swollen center.

"I like being there, too, but it's hard to touch you. Now I can do whatever I want," she says. I don't disagree. Instead, I put my hand on top of hers and press her into me. She is unleashing a side of me that I don't recognize. Her fingertips massage my swollen clit through my pants and in a move of desperation, I slide my pants down to my knees just enough to give her access. My panties are still on, but that doesn't deter her. She pulls them to the side and I gasp when she slips two fingers inside of me. She's not gentle and it's such a turn on. I greedily push my hips into her, my body torn between the pleasure of her touch and the pain of her slamming into me. I claw for release, pull her into me, and push her away again. She breaks the kiss to move down my body, her tongue finding the waistband of my panties. She tugs on my hips and I lift myself just enough for her to pull the panties down. I cry out when I feel her warm mouth envelop my throbbing clit, the relief almost instantaneous, the build-up inevitable. My pants prevent me from spreading my legs, but that doesn't slow Kerry down. Her fingers find my pussy again while her hot mouth focuses on my clit. I crash into my orgasm hard and fast, not stopping until I come again. She slows down when she feels my legs shake, knowing I can't take any more. She gently pushes my legs down and stretches out beside me. I can't look at her. I need to catch my breath and try hard not to dissect what just happened. She is quiet beside me, her hand resting on my stomach, waiting for me.

"I love Irish sunrises," I say, finally finding my voice. It's a little hoarse from my constant moaning and the cold air. I feel her body vibrate as she softly laughs. She lifts her head to look at me. I reach up and touch her face.

"Did you even look out from beneath the blanket?" she asks, placing a soft kiss on my lips. I peek out for a moment, then throw the blanket back over my head.

"It's gorgeous," I say. "And very bright."

"It really is beautiful. I'm sorry you missed it."

"I'm not sorry at all. My view was so much better." I have no idea where my confidence is coming from. I roll toward her so that we are face to face. "What an incredible day." She nods and links her fingers with mine.

"Definitely one of my favorites," she says. She leans into me and I hold her. We fit well together.

"Are you tired?" I ask.

"I don't know what I am. I'm tired, excited, happy. We've been up almost twenty-four hours straight," she says, looking at her watch.

"Let's go back to the apartment. We can catch a nap. Unless you want to get back to the hospital." I don't want to be presumptuous.

"That actually sounds fantastic," she says. She pops her head out to look at the sunrise. "It really is gorgeous."

"I told you," I say.

"I believe I told you," she says. She hands me my blouse and watches me dress, placing a quick kiss on my stomach before I button it up. The air is cold, and crisp, and I shiver when Kerry removes the blanket from around us. "Let's get out of here." We waste no time grabbing our coats and getting back down to the car. I take a quick moment to look around in the light. It really would have been beautiful to watch the sunrise from up here, but I wouldn't change what just happened for any sunrise anywhere.

Abram greets us at the door when we finally reach the shop. I scoop him up and bring him upstairs. The adrenaline is gone and I can't wait to sleep. I head to the bathroom to clean up a bit and throw on a long T-shirt. Kerry is already in bed. I slide between the covers and mold myself against her, surprised that she is completely naked. As much as I want to touch her all over, exhaustion settles over us, and we fall asleep almost instantly.

Chapter Thirteen

I wake up to an empty bed, but I can hear Kerry somewhere in the apartment. It sounds like she is softly singing and I lean over enough to see out of the bedroom door. She is holding Abram like a baby and singing him a lullaby. She is wearing a shirt of mine and her panties. I liked it better when she was naked. I flop back on the bed even though we've been asleep for five hours. I'm still tired so I close my eyes and try to squeeze a few more minutes of rest in. It isn't long before I feel Kerry's warm hands massage my legs and I shamelessly spread myself for her. She runs her tongue up the side of my thigh, then skips over to the other one to do the same. It's delicious torture.

"I'm pretty sure it's my turn," I say.

"It's whoever is on top." She slides me to the end of the bed and hooks the back of my knees over her shoulders. That gets me to open my eyes. She smiles devilishly at me. The second her tongue touches my slit, I close my eyes again. She takes her time, running her tongue up and down my folds, her arms wrapped around my legs so that I can't buck against her for more friction. I'm not going to fight her on whose turn it is. If she wants to fuck me again, I'm not going to stop her. I'm only here a few more hours so I'm going to make the most of them. I relax because I don't want to come right away. It happened too quickly this morning and I don't want to embarrass myself again. This time I focus on her, the way she commands my body's responses with only her touch. She releases my legs, but I keep them there. I like this position. She slips two fingers inside of me and I moan in appreciation. Her movements are slow at first, building me up gently with every slight thrust. My juices start flowing and my hips start moving when she slides a third finger inside of me. I want to spread myself to accommodate her, but if I do, I will lose this angle and the depth she is able to hit. This feels too good to stop.

"You sound so incredibly sexy," she says. I open my eyes to find her staring at me. She looks away only to watch her fingers glide in and out of me. "And you are so tight and delicious." She leans forward, my knees sliding off of her shoulders, her fingers still inside of me, and kisses me passionately. Her hand moves faster and I grip her shoulders and hold on as she pushes me into another orgasm. I'm loud and I don't care if anyone hears me. I shake with the aftershocks and, after a few minutes, stretch my legs and relax.

"You are..." I say, not really knowing how to finish the sentence. I don't want to insult her, but I want her to know that I haven't felt this good in a long time. "Amazing." That sums it up.

"And you are..." She kisses me soundly. "Wonderful." I wasn't expecting that. She curls up next to me and I run my fingertips across her back, completely lost in my thoughts. What a terrible time to have sex. I have to be at the airport in less than ten hours and I will probably never be back. I don't feel regret; I feel lonely. Or maybe it's sadness. I feel like I'm missing a fantastic opportunity with somebody who isn't like anybody I've ever dated before. She's stubborn, borderline rude, yet extremely passionate, beautiful, loving, and caring. She drives me crazy in good and bad ways. I stroke her hair and now that I'm relaxed, decide it's my turn to do delicious things to her body. I roll on top of her, stretching her legs out with mine and pushing her arms above her head. She smiles at me. "Whatever are you going to do to me, Grace Danner?"

I kiss her, softly at first, until I feel her body respond underneath me. I feel her nipples harden with excitement. I can't believe she still has clothes on. I slide the T-shirt up until her breasts peek out from beneath the hem. Her pale pink nipples are erect and beg for attention. I suck one into my mouth and she exhales sharply. The texture of the areola against the smoothness of her perfect breast is heaven in my mouth.

"I'm not going to last." She runs her hands through my hair, holding me close to her.

"I don't want you to." I move my mouth to give her other nipple the same attention. I'm trying to take my time with her, but I can't wait to taste her so I slide down and am rewarded with a very wet and very warm pussy. I waste no time getting to know her body and hungrily run my tongue up and down the soft pleats, pressing my mouth hard against her. She squirms and releases the sexiest moan I have ever heard when I slip inside of her. I moan with her out of sheer desire to fuck her. She raises her hips up to meet my every thrust, inhaling sharply the deeper I go. Still inside of her, I climb up the bed to rest between her legs, my hand between us, still moving. I want to kiss her. I want to hear her when she comes. She digs her fingertips into my back, then my hips as she pulls me into her with every thrust of my hand. She breaks the kiss as the first quivers of the impending orgasm wash over her. I feel her walls clench my fingers with need. Her legs start shaking and she makes a deep growling noise that turns into a loud, gravelly groan. She writhes into me, clutches me, and takes every bit of pleasure from this moment. It's a beautiful experience with her. I slowly remove my hand and press myself closer to her.

"You're beautiful when you come." I kiss from her neck to her ear and tug the soft lobe between my teeth. She catches her breath when I bite down.

"Mmm. We should have done this sooner," she says.

"You didn't like me."

"If I knew you were capable of this, I would have forgiven you on day one," she says. "Do you really have to leave tonight?" I've been thinking about that since she started undressing me on top of the cliff. I should be in Dallas for the client on Sunday. My boss did reach out to me. But is my presence necessary?

"Well, I guess I could change my flight to Saturday. That would give us a couple more days if you're serious about wanting to spend time with me."

"That would be fantastic. But I don't want you to get into trouble on account of me."

"I honestly don't know why the boss is so desperate for me to be there. She can certainly handle it. Plus Alisa is more than capable." I lean down to kiss her. "I'll e-mail them in a bit."

"You should do it now, Grace. What we do over the next several hours will depend on their answer. As a matter of fact, you should text her instead." Good idea. I'm anxious to find out what else Kerry has in store for us today. "Why don't I run out and grab us some food? Maybe by the time I get back, you'll have an answer." I don't want to leave her warm body, but my stomach is growling so I relent.

"Okay. But hurry back." She kisses me and jumps out of bed. I watch her dress, appreciating her tall, lithe body with her firm, small breasts and the thin strip of red hair nestled above my new favorite part of her body.

"Do you have any questions? Is there anything that you are concerned about or are you all set?" I ask Alisa. I asked my boss if I could bow out of the dinner plans Sunday and just be back in the office later that week. She wasn't happy, but understands that I need more time. She knows I have only taken one vacation in the past eight years and that one was three years ago when the ex-girlfriend and I just started getting serious about our relationship.

"No, I think I've got everything. Find out Beck's needs, wants, and desires. Plus Morgan and her assistant will be there," Alisa says.

"Don't let them get crazy. Just write everything down. I trust you. Call me if you need me." I jump online and once again, change my flight. Instead of a late flight out tonight, I switch it to midday on Tuesday. That gives me four full days with Kerry.

"I sure hope you're hungry," Kerry says as she swings through the front door with four bags of groceries in her arms.

"Starving. I've been working up an appetite."

"Without me?"

"What did you get us?" I walk over to peek into the bags.

"Everything because strangely, I, too, worked up an appetite." She pulls out bread, meat, cheese, vegetables, a pie, cookies, and some paper plates and napkins. "I had to get items that don't require utensils or real plates since you've donated all of that to the charity store." Good thinking.

"This should tide us over until dinner. And I checked with my boss. She said I don't have to be back until next week so I changed my flight for Tuesday." Kerry doesn't say anything, but instead, leans over and kisses me hard. "Have you checked on Emma and Ian?" I ask.

"Mum said they are doing well and resting. I would like to go see them tonight if you're up for it," she says.

"You do what you want and need to do."

"No, I mean, would you like to go up there with me?" she asks.

"Yes, but no. I want you to spend time with your family. Don't worry about me." The last thing I want to do is be clingy after sex. I decide to play this cool. "I have tons of work I can get caught up on while you are visiting with them." I really don't, but I can surf the web for cute cat videos. Abram might even like that. "Plus, I can take a nap. I didn't really get a lot of sleep the past thirty hours or so."

"Yeah, I could use a little bit more sleep, too." She fixes us sandwiches and we sit down on the couch to eat a late lunch. "I'm happy you aren't leaving tonight. I get you for four more days."

I can't help but smile. "Promise me you won't worry about me. Do what you normally would do if I wasn't here."

"But you are here, and I want to spend time with you. I will plan out a few fun things to do, but still give us time," she says. I would be perfectly fine just holing up here until Tuesday.

"We will figure things out." Feeling stuffed, I put my plate on the coffee table and stretch out on the couch. Kerry puts a pillow on her lap and pats it for me to put my legs on the pillow. She softly runs her hands up and down my legs, stroking them. I know she's doing it to be kind, but I'm so turned on right now. After the third stifled moan, I finally throw in the towel.

"That feels so good." I close my eyes and just allow the pleasure of her touch to take over. She runs her fingertips up near my boy shorts and I automatically relax my legs so that they spread apart slightly. She doesn't disappoint. She runs her hands up to the edge, hesitates for just a moment, then presses her hand against my core, causing me to moan. She runs her thumb up and down my slit.

"You're already so wet," she says.

"I've been like this since we got here." She smiles at me, but continues to massage, pressing harder and harder with each stroke. I move one of my legs down to the floor so that she has full access to me. I lift my hips up and push against her hand, wanting more, needing more. She crawls above me until we are face to face. Her body is above mine, but not touching. I reach for her hips and pull them to rest against me. She fits me so well.

"Why do I have a feeling we aren't going to leave this apartment for a long, long time?" she asks right before her lips capture mine in a kiss. I moan my answer. When she relaxes completely against me, I tilt my hips up and circle her waist with my legs.

"You know, for being so thin, you are surprisingly strong," I say. She places tiny kisses on my face until she reaches my neck. I buck when her mouth finds the sensitive spot right above my collarbone and moan with appreciation. I stop talking when she slides her body down mine and I can feel her hot breath against my thigh.

"You should stay naked the entire time we are here." She pulls my shorts off. Her mouth touches my slit before I am settled back on the couch and I cry out in surprise. She presses my knees together and buries her face in my thighs, her tongue barely touching my clit. Not enough to make me come, but enough to drive me crazy with need. I raise my hips into her, hoping she will press harder, but she doesn't and I am forced to accept that she wants to tease me for now. The minute I relax, she releases my legs and spreads me open. I put one leg on the back of the couch and my other foot back on the floor. I try not to move against her mouth, but I can't help it. I stop short of putting my hand on the back of her head.

"Please, Kerry." I hate that I can't wait. She stops.

"You rush entirely too much. I promise I won't let you down." She maintains eye contact while running her tongue from the bottom of my slit to the top. My body jerks at the intimacy. She runs her hands up my thighs and holds my hips in place. She is firm and I writhe against her, not to get away, but to see how rough she is willing to be with me. She doesn't disappoint and I feel myself getting wetter with every flick of her tongue, every bruising squeeze of her fingertips into my thighs. When I hear her moan, I grind myself against her for release. She stops short several times, bringing me to the edge, then waiting until I settle down. I want to be frustrated, I want release, but I also want to know how far she can take me. After the fifth time, she slides two fingers inside of me, then three. I arch off the couch and come fiercely, my orgasm exploding. It takes me a while to catch my breath. Kerry crawls back up my body, her body still heavy with desire. "Let's get back to the bed." I nod, but don't move. I can't move. She stands in front of me. "Do you need a moment? Or maybe an incentive?" I watch as she slowly unbuttons her blouse and pulls it from her slacks. Her slacks fall in a heap on the floor and she stands before me wearing a lacy bra with matching panties, her blouse hanging low on the back of her smooth shoulders. I reach out for her, but she avoids me and offers her hand instead. "We need to go to the bedroom. There are delicious things I want to do to you and I can't do them here." The muscles in my legs start working and I make the effort to stand. She pulls me quickly against her, the rough lace of her bra and panties rubbing against my sensitive skin in the most exciting way.

"Tell me again why we waited so long to do this?" I ask right before her mouth captures mine in a mind blowing kiss. I forget my question as she pulls me to the bedroom. I don't even notice when she completely undresses me, or when we hit the bed. I can only feel her hard, lean body flush against me and her full lips devouring my mouth.

Chapter Fourteen

The sun is bright and because I was too busy touching and being touched all night, I forgot to close the blinds. It's early. Too early. Kerry's head is on my shoulder, her body mostly under the covers. One of her long legs is curled up over the blanket and I reach down to stroke it gently. What a whirlwind the last forty-eight hours have been. This whole entire trip has been crazy. It's funny how I have no desire to hurry back to my life in Dallas. In the past, I was antsy to get back to the comfort of my work whether I was out on assignment, on a short weekend getaway, or even when I did take that vacation three years ago with she-who-shall-not-be-named.

"Is it time to get up?" Kerry croaks out. I squeeze her leg.

"No. I forgot to pull the blinds. It's still early. Go back to sleep."

"Tell Abram to close the blinds," she says. She's quiet as I stroke her hair. I think she's fallen asleep, but she quietly sighs with pleasure. "This is nice."

I smile. "I like your hair. It's one of the first things that attracted me to you." I can feel her smile against me.

"It's so wild and untamed," she says.

"It's beautiful. As soon as you jumped out of your car to verbally assault me on our first day, I couldn't take my eyes off of it. And even when we weren't talking, I would always go back to it in my mind."

She pinches my side, causing me to laugh. "Verbally assaulted? I was keeping my anger in check."

"I don't know that I could handle your anger at full force," I say.

"It's not that bad. If I'm really upset, I get really quiet."

"Good to know. I won't get on your bad side. Again."

"You really weren't on it in the first place. It's my fault. I'm just in a bad spot," she says.

"Look at it this way. Selling the shop helps The Mulligan Group out, not just you. Your commission will be good, but the family gets a portion, too. And let's not talk about it, okay? Let's enjoy the day. What do you want to do today?" I ask, trying to keep her mind off of our situation.

"I'd like to see Emma and Ian. Oh, and Keagan," she says. I laugh.

"That sounds like a good idea. When do they get to go home? Do you know?" I ask.

"Probably tomorrow."

That surprises me. "Wow. Back home, most new mothers go home within twenty-four hours," I say.

"How are new mothers going to know how to take care of the baby after only a few hours?" she asks. She raises her head to look up at me, the incredulous look on her face hard to miss. "Seriously. That doesn't even make sense to me." Now that I think about it, it doesn't make sense to me either.

I shrug because I don't have the answer. "It does seem rather quick, huh? Well, why don't you spend some time with your family today? I can run down to the wharf and take some pics and look around."

"Wait, you don't want to go with me?" she asks. My heart flutters. I feel my emotions pull me in every direction. My soul pushes me toward her, toward her life and family, while my mind pushes me away from her, away from this life in Ireland.

"I don't think I belong there. Thank you for thinking of me though. It's not a problem for me to do my own thing. Really." I smile at her, hoping it will lessen the blow.

"You belong with me and nobody will say anything. Everybody likes you, Grace," she says. My heart quivers again at the thought of being hers. "Plus, where else will you see such baby perfection?" She's so convincing, but I stay strong. I can't fall for this girl. Nothing good will come from this. This is supposed to be an extended weekend of fun and really good sex. The kind of sex you think about weeks, months, years later, and blush from just the memories. I've never been this open and free with any other woman before. Maybe it's because I know the chances of seeing her again are slim and I'm giving myself to her completely. I consciously ignore the tugging on my heart that happens every time I look at her or when she moves closer to me.

"It's okay. I already said my good-byes to everybody yesterday. I'll feel like a stray dog hanging around," I say.

She laughs. "They'll be happy for me that you've extended your trip. When I'm happy, the family is happy."

"So, I make you happy?" I ask.

She leans up and kisses me soundly. "Very much."

"Strange how all of this has happened." I press my lips against hers again. "One minute you hate that I'm here, now you don't mind it."

"It's strictly because you give me really good orgasms," she says.

I laugh. "That's it? Huh. Weird because I've never been accused of that before."

"That's just crazy. You're beautiful, passionate, submissive, everything I like in a woman," she says. I shiver when she says I'm submissive. She's managed to tap into a side of me I didn't know I even had. All this time I've been playing the role of aggressor when I needed somebody in control of me. "And why are you getting out of this bed?"

"I need to leave you alone so you can get up and go to the hospital," I say. She reaches my wrists before I climb off of the bed.

"It's still really early. Neither one of us needs to be anywhere just yet. Wait. That's not true. You need to be right here."

"You're insatiable, but I love it," I say right before I slide back on the bed and spend the next hour getting to know her even better.

Chapter Fifteen

"I can't believe you're still there." It's good to hear Morgan's voice. It's been too long.

"I should have just taken two weeks from the beginning so that I wouldn't feel so bad about it now." I'm frustrated with my boss and myself. We both know I never say no to a job, so I don't know what happens next. "Has she said anything to you?"

"Nothing really, other than she's surprised you haven't wrapped things up yet. She knows we're friends. She isn't going to talk shit about you in front of me," Morgan says. "It's not as if Alisa can't get things done in your absence. Enough about all of this." In my mind, I can picture her waving her hands dramatically at me to get my mind off of it. "Tell me all about your fire hot girlfriend." She always makes me laugh.

"She's great. Right now she's with her family for a bit, but I'm sure once she gets back here, it will be game on," I say.

"You needed this trip, Grace," Morgan says. "You sound, I don't know how to describe it. Happy? Stronger? I don't think I've ever heard you so relaxed before."

I smile just thinking of Kerry. "This is exactly what I needed."

"Great sex? Hot body? Did she show you things you only ever dreamed about?" I know Morgan is joking, but my breath hitches when I think about how she topped me on the couch. I shiver recalling our exchange and how she let me know she was in control. "Hey, did I lose you? Are you still there?"

"Yeah, I'm here. I just had to...um...Abram the cat was getting into something." She doesn't need to know explicit details. Mind blowing sex is good enough for her. She doesn't need to know that I can feel myself slipping and how something inside of me tightens up whenever I see Kerry or think about her.

"What are you going to do with him?" she asks.

I stroke his ear and smile as he purrs for me. "I guess Leigh is going to take him in. Although she has a really big dog that I know is going to drive him insane. Emma just had the baby so she can't handle a cat, too. And Conor, he already told me his dad would not let him have a pet. I just feel bad for this little lover. I'm going to miss him," I say.

"Maybe when you get home, you should really think about adopting a cat from the shelter." Not a bad idea, but I'm afraid I will get a crazy one. My track record for any kind of companion hasn't been good.

"I'll think about it. I just need to get through all of this first. Kerry's dad thinks the shop will sell quickly. It's in a prime location and even though the economy isn't great, some big company will probably get it at a decent price."

"Does that bother you? I mean, shouldn't you get the most bang for your buck?" she asks.

"Yes, but a part of me wants it done already. It's exhausting here. I struggle with wanting to be friends with these wonderful people, and then turning around and laying them off. My aunt must have been crazy when she concocted this idea," I say.

"Just think, you'll have a life changing amount of money. You can do anything you want. Buy anything you want. It will be great," Morgan says. I frown. Maybe three weeks ago that was the plan, but right now, it's just not sitting well with me.

"I know. I just need to get on that plane Tuesday morning and never look back," I say.

That gives me three full days with Kerry. She already told me she is taking me to the airport. I hang up with Morgan and decide I need to go for a walk. I've been cooped up in the apartment far too long and fresh air will do me some good. I want to walk through town one last time since I have a few hours to kill. The sun is shining after a quick rain shower this morning, so I grab a small umbrella, my camera, and a few slices of bread to feed the fish and seagulls on the wharf. I'm surprised to see Colleen down on one of the boats. Her out of control hair is pulled back in a clip, the bright color and curls hard to miss. I recognize her by her hair before I even see her face. She waves at me.

"Colleen, good morning. Do you ever sleep?" I ask. She smiles.

"I have to make sure my husband and my boys are working," she says. "Or else we won't have anything for lunch today. Boys, say hello to Grace. She's Nola's niece from America." All three boys and her husband immediately stop what they are doing to say hello. I'm impressed. She obviously runs that household.

"It's nice to meet you. Are you going back out?" I ask. I don't know the schedules or when the best time to catch fish is.

"Oh, we've already put in a full day. We're going to get the fish back to the restaurant, help clean them up and then get cleaned up ourselves," Colleen's husband says.

"Do you mind if I take a few pictures of you working on the boat?" I ask. This isn't something I see back home.

"Hop on. Boys, fix your hair," Colleen scolds them.

"Oh, it's fine. They look great," I say. They all have windblown hair, suntanned faces even though it's only April, and are full of muscles. One of the boys reaches out his hand to help me on the boat, ensuring I'm steady before letting my hand go. Colleen tells me they are eighteen, twenty-one, and twenty-three years old. I can tell they are hard workers.

"Do you have any daughters?" I ask Colleen.

"Clara. She's at the restaurant now."

"Does she work there full time?" I ask.

"Oh, no. She goes to school in the afternoons, but helps out in the morning at the restaurant."

"I love that your entire family is involved in your business," I say. She looks at me strangely, like this is normal and she's confused as to why I would point out the obvious. I slip away and happily snap photos of all four men working on their haul. It's beautifully mechanical how well they operate together. They are quiet, efficient, and know each other's moves. After about ten minutes on the boat, I thank everybody and tell them I will definitely have lunch or dinner at their restaurant again before I leave. I find my meditation rock from last week and sit on it, happy to be at peace. I feed the fish pieces of bread and throw some crumbs on a nearby rock. The seagulls seem tame enough that I could probably reach out and touch one, but I don't just in case they decide to peck my eyes out. I don't even know how long I have been sitting on this rock. I watch several boats glide into the harbor and some sail away. Off in the distance, a lone figure walks toward me. I know it's Kerry. I recognize her tall, lithe frame and beautiful red hair. Ever since I told her that it's beautiful, she has been wearing it down for me. My heart speeds up the closer she gets, the flutter fast and furious in my chest. It's welcoming and frightening at the same time. She smiles and a jolt of energy circulates through my body.

"Why did I know you would be here?" she asks right before she kisses the corner of my mouth.

"Hi. What a nice surprise to see you here," I say. She helps me off of the rock, but doesn't let my hand go when we are on the boardwalk. She laces her fingers with mine and we stroll along the water's edge. I give her fingers a tiny squeeze and she squeezes mine back. I smile at that small, yet meaningful gesture of affection.

"Did you get a lot of pictures?"

I nod. "This is such a wonderful place. No wonder my aunt picked Howth to live in and start a business."

"I love Howth. I love Dublin, too. Your aunt was a smart woman," she says.

"Tell me about her," I say. Kerry squeezes my fingers gently, her warm hand comforting to me.

"She was always so nice to everybody. The Irish Garden was her dream come true. She loved flowers, loved making people smile, and truly loved her life. Did you know she was a trickster?" I shake my head no. "She made that place so much fun for Emma, Leigh, and Conor, and made them all feel like they were a family. Even when she was diagnosed with her cancer, she still had a positive attitude."

"I never even knew she was sick. I mean, my family never said anything to me. Of course, I should have made the effort to get to know her," I say.

"Don't beat yourself up, Grace. It's not your fault. She was in a completely different country and you were busy building up your career," Kerry says. Yeah, that doesn't help me at all.

"I'm so selfish. I can't help compare our lives, Kerry. We are so very different. You are all about your family and heritage, and I'm all about myself. I'm shallow, my friends are shallow, hell, even my job is shallow," I say.

"Stop. You are not. You love Morgan so she can't be shallow. You've worked so hard to get where you are. People depend on you and your talents. Don't think I don't know about your late night e-mails and projects. That makes your job not shallow. We are just different people who grew up differently. I know what's in your heart. I know the real you, even if only for a little bit." I walk with Kerry, my voice silent, but my thoughts loud and disruptive to me. "Quit thinking so much. Let's go grab a late lunch or early supper, then get back to the apartment. I only have you for a few days." She ends the sentence with a frown, so I reach up and place a small kiss in the corner of the frown, my tongue quickly touching her lips.

Chapter Sixteen

There is a different feel to the apartment today. The heaviness of me leaving tomorrow hangs between us. Even Abram is more active, walking back and forth.

"Are you sure Leigh is all right with watching him?" I ask when Abram jumps up on the couch and curls up next to us.

"She promises she is."

"But what about Danga? He's even bigger than I am," I say.

"Don't let his size fool you. Abram will have complete control of that household by the end of the week. And I promise you that if it doesn't work out with Leigh, I'll be the backup stepmom. Once this place sells, I can get my place and Abram can move in with me and the goats. He will love it." She brings my hand up to her lips to give it a quick kiss. I'm really going to miss Kerry and Abram.

"I know you will love him and take care of him. I trust you," I say. I try to give her an encouraging smile, but it comes out sad and I'm surprised at the sting in my eyes. I quickly look down at Abram and play with his ears, hoping she doesn't see my tears. If she notices, she doesn't call me out.

"He will be king of my farm. Hey, what do you want to do on our last day?"

I want to spend the day in bed with her. I want to memorize her curves and touch her everywhere. I want to taste her skin and feel her warmth against me. "Honestly? I want you. I just want this final day to be about us."

She leans over and kisses me softly. "That sounds fantastic. I was hoping you would say something delicious like that." The gleam in her eye tells me that she's going to make this a very memorable day for me and I shiver with anticipation.

"Can I just say how much I've enjoyed this last week with you? Thank you for spending it with me. I know you are busy with baby Ian and you are sacrificing your time with him, and your job, to be with me." I pull her close to me and give her a quick kiss on her mouth. "So thank you." I barely get the words out before she pushes me back down on the couch, giving Abram just enough time to scoot away or risk getting squashed beneath us. I break the kiss first. "As much as I enjoyed our last make out session on the couch, I think I'd much rather be on the bed."

"Okay, but under one condition," she says, pulling me up with her.

"Anything for you," I say. I mean it.

She raises her thick eyebrow at me. "You can't say something like that without knowing first," she says.

"I trust you." I stand still while she peppers my face with tiny kisses and unbuttons my jeans. I help her and take off my sweater and camisole, but leave my bra on. I'm so thankful that I packed only matching bra and panty sets. The look of lust and appreciation in her eyes empowers me. I reach out to her, but she steps out of my reach.

"No," she says. I pout. She runs her fingertips over my mouth and gasps slightly when I suck her finger into my mouth. Her lips part as she watches me, her breath warm against my mouth.

"I love watching you," I say.

She smiles at me. "Watching me do what?"

"The way you look when you're turned on. Your eyes darken and you get this little smirk on your face knowing that we're about to have mind-blowing sex." I keep it lighthearted because if I don't, I will crumble.

"Mind-blowing sex?" she asks. I nod. "Not sweet love making or a grand opportunity to get to know each other better physically?" I shrug like it's no big deal. She takes a step closer to me so that our bodies are only an inch apart. I can feel her heat without touching her.

"Can I touch you now?" I ask. I lick my lips wanting to taste her skin, her mouth, her sex. She disappoints me by shaking her head. I sigh. "What would you like?"

"I want you to watch me," she says. She slowly unbuttons her blouse, her eyes never leaving mine. I feel like the first one to look away, submits. I want to, but a part of me wants to hold on for a bit longer, to challenge her a bit. I don't want to give in right away, even though we both know I will. My peripheral can only pick up so much before I have to break eye contact so I can watch her shrug out of her blouse. Her skin is so pale and smooth and I have to ball my hands into fists so that I don't pull her to me. Her flat, tight stomach, the one I feathered with light kisses last night, is now bare to me. She isn't wearing a bra and her nipples are hard and puckered, beckoning for attention.

"Please let me touch you," I beg. She shakes her head no. A cocky smile slides into place. She knows she just won. I stand there and wait for her to tell me what she wants. I moan when her pants slide to the floor. She is now standing in front of me in only silky panties. I can't help but drop to my knees in front of her. I'm weak with desire. My mouth is inches from her. I can already tell she is wet for me. I lean forward and place a delicate kiss on her thigh. She doesn't stop me. I stop myself from smiling because if she sees me, she might stop me and I don't think I can. I lean over and place a kiss on the other thigh. She spreads her stance making it easier for me. She still hasn't stopped me. I slip my tongue under her panties and lick the silky spot where her thigh meets the softest skin near her sex. My tongue is demanding, yet her panties are still in the way. I need my hands. She surprises me when she reaches down and moves her panties to the side giving me full access. We make eye contact and I keep looking at her as I run my tongue up her slit, stopping at her clit. I apply more pressure at the top and she moans. I break eye contact first.

"May I please use my hands?" I ask. She shakes her head no again. I'm not deterred. As a matter of fact, I like this challenge. I lean forward more and bury my face into her mound. My tongue digs into her folds and I taste her warm wetness, the tangy sweetness only makes me want her more. I feel her hand on the back of my head, moving me closer and holding me tighter against her body. She starts to sway and I can feel the slight vibration of her shaky legs. I really don't want her to come this soon. "Now may I use my hands?"

She looks down at me, her eyes narrow slits, her mouth partly open. I watch her swallow hard. The second she nods, I rip off her panties and push her back on the bed. I guide her legs up so that her knees are to her chest and hold them there as I continue to lick her. I'm bold. I run my tongue low, feeling the curve of her ass before I move back up to capture her clit in my mouth. She cries out and starts moving her hips up against me, anxious for more friction. I need more. I release her legs, and she surprises me by keeping them there. I easily slip two fingers inside of her, as deep as I can go, and moan as she moans. She is tight, but quickly accommodates me. I run my tongue up her slit and suck her clit back into my mouth. I'm not gentle and she doesn't want me to be. She puts her feet back down on the bed and spreads her knees as far apart as they will go. I am half standing between her legs, and half lying on the bed, drilling my fingers into her. She grabs the back of my head again and holds me against her as her orgasm takes over. I love how open she is. It's morning, full light, and she is spread wide open for me. My hand is cramping, my legs are strained, and my face is covered with her, but I'm smiling and she is laughing. Today is perfect.

❖

We head for Sullivan's for one last early dinner. Kerry holds my hand as we walk down to the restaurant. Her conversation is light and I know she's just trying to keep our minds off of tomorrow. Today was entirely for me. We stayed in the apartment all day, barely clothed, ravenous for each other. And food. Eventually, we cave and decide to eat.

"What's been your favorite part about your trip?" she asks.

I don't hesitate. "You." Her fingers squeeze mine.

"Besides me. Tell me what you like about Ireland?"

"I love how beautiful it is here. I love that I don't even know what year it is. Everybody is so friendly and even though I've only been here a short time, I feel like I'm already a part of this town."

"That's why I love it here, too. I'm sure it's like this all over the world, but this is my home," she says.

I get a crazy idea in my head. "Hey, when life slows a bit for you and your family, why don't you come visit me for a long weekend? I know you can't take a lot of time, but I would like to show you my home. You like big cities and Dallas is pretty big. Come visit me. Next month." I watch her process my offer. She doesn't say no right away so I press on. "Take a Friday and Monday off. Come spend them with me. You can catch a red-eye out Thursday night and be back Tuesday." I almost melt when she nods.

"I'd like to see your life and where you live," she says. I refrain from skipping all the way down to Colleen's restaurant and whooping out my excitement. Instead I smile at Kerry.

"I promise to make it a great trip. We will even squeeze in some sightseeing."

"Do you live in the actual city?"

"Yes. I have a condo close to my work."

"Obviously, you'll have to show me where you work, too," she says. We reach Sullivan's and Kerry opens the door for me. Colleen fusses over us immediately and pushes us into a private booth.

"I thought for sure you weren't going to make it," she says. I don't know if she's scolding me or not. She's always so animated that it's hard to tell.

"Come on, Colleen. I told you I would. You have such a beautiful family. It was amazing to watch them work." She shrugs me off, but I can see the pride in her eyes. "So, what do you recommend as my final meal here?"

"Our Shepherd's Pie is outstanding. I don't believe you've had that yet," she says. Kerry nods so we order two and beers. Colleen runs off to get our orders and Kerry reaches out for my hand.

"I never even got to cook for you," Kerry says.

"Well, if you really, really want to, you can cook for me when you visit," I say. I know I won't cook so I'm running through all of my favorite restaurants in town that I can take Kerry to or at least order take-out from.

"Will I be able to find all the ingredients I need?" she asks. I smile at her.

"Everything is big in Texas, including the grocery stores," I say. She doesn't get my joke. I sober up. "There are several stores near me. I guarantee you will be able to find what you need."

"Let's see when a good weekend would be." She pulls out her phone. I tell her Memorial Day weekend, but I don't think I can wait a month to see her and touch her again. It turns out that she can come the weekend before and I agree without even looking at my schedule.

"I've been to America a time or two," Colleen sets our plates down in front of us, knowing exactly what we are up to. "It's very different from here. But not in a bad way. I had a good time visiting, but home always calls me back." She winks at us and leaves.

"I promise to show you a good time." I can see uncertainty in Kerry's eyes and try my best to set her mind at ease. "We can go see a baseball game, maybe a concert if anybody great is in town. The food is phenomenal and there is always something to do. Or we can just hang out at my place. I'm easy." That makes her smile. "Well, you know what I mean." Her smile gets bigger. I shake my head at her. I like how sexually free I feel with Kerry. I like her energy, her passion, her anger, and her heart. I get closer and closer to her every time I'm with her.

"What are you thinking about?" she asks.

"Why?"

"Because you have such a sweet look on your face right now."

"I'm thinking about us and how I've enjoyed our time together." She doesn't answer me, but smiles back instead. "And this is really good." I poke my fork at my dinner, hoping to change the subject. Perhaps I've said too much.

"Colleen really knows what she's doing in the kitchen. You're going to miss her cooking," Kerry says.

"Without a doubt, but I'd like to fit in my clothes again. I probably have gained five pounds since I've been here."

Kerry looks me up and down and lifts an eyebrow. "I think you look great. Maybe you needed the five pounds," she says.

"Well, thank you, but my wardrobe is based on my figure before Ireland, not after. I don't want to have to go out and buy all new clothes. After today, I'm back to salads and proteins," I say, frowning at the thought. "Plus, I'm sure I'll be so busy at work that I won't eat regular meals."

"I hope that you won't be working so hard when I visit," she says.

"I promise I won't even think about work while you are with me. It will be you and only you."

"Hurry up and finish your meal. I only have you for a few more hours and I plan to make the most of them." We don't talk a lot after that statement. I drink my beer, take a few more bites of my meal. When I push my plate away, Kerry jumps up, throws money on the table, grabs my hands, and pulls me to her. "Let's go."

"Don't you ladies want dessert?" Colleen asks. Shit. I need to tell Colleen thank you.

"Oh, no. I'm full. Thank you. The food was delicious. I have to go pack tonight. Thank you so much for everything. Your hospitality, your kindness, and your excellent food. This is a fantastic pub you have here." I walk into her outstretched arms for a hug.

"Take care of yourself, Gracie. It was nice to meet you. Hopefully, you will be back to our small town?" I shrug.

"That would be nice," I say. Kerry reaches out and I slip my hand in hers. It's our time now. If things go really well, then maybe I will be back for a visit now and then. I wave to the people I've come to know in the short time I've been here. Back home, if I saw the same people in a bar night after night, I would feel sorry for them. Here, I see everybody as a family. We get back to the shop in very little time and Kerry surprises me by wanting to go up to the rooftop. She takes a moment to turn on the patio heat lamp that instantly warms us.

"You haven't really experienced the rooftop at night, have you?" She pulls me into her arms. She turns me around so that we are both looking out at the Irish Sea.

"How could I have forgotten about this wonderful place?" I shiver, not because I'm cold, but because she is warm.

"You've been busy. Plus, I've been stealing you away."

"Like I'm going to complain about that," I say. She folds her arms across my chest and starts nuzzling my neck from behind. I tilt my head to give her better access. She scrapes her teeth across my skin and chills break out across my body. I shiver again.

"Are you cold?" she asks. She knows I'm not and it's her touch that's driving me crazy. My body is on fire. My nipples are hard, my clit is throbbing all from thirty seconds of being in her arms.

"You know the answer to that." I try to turn back around, but she tightens her grip.

"Don't move." I still immediately. She loosens her grip when she feels I have surrendered to her. She unbuttons my blouse from behind, exposing me to the cool night air. My nipples tighten painfully at her touch and I try to press myself into her, but she steps back. She turns me back to face her. "What do you want to do tonight?"

"I want to be in control." I'm shaking partly because of the cold and partly because I know she will say yes to me.

"Whatever you want," she says. I wish we had more time. I wish I didn't have to leave tomorrow. Being in control of her, of us, is the best gift she could give me. I move a chair closer to the heat lamp.

"Sit." She immediately obliges. I should have had her undress first, but I will try to make it interesting this way, too. I grab the blanket and put it around my shoulders. I reach for a cushion and throw it on the ground in front of her. She smiles. I rub my hands over her knees and spread them apart. She nestles down on the chair. I massage her legs and gently work my way up the apex of her thighs. She moans softly. I slowly unbutton her pants and lean forward to place tiny kisses across the top of her mound and the skin right above her panties. I pull her zipper down with my teeth, stopping only to place tiny, wet kisses knowing she can feel my tongue through the silk and lace. She reaches down to put her hands in my hair. "No," I say. She briefly smiles and drops her hands to her sides. "Lift up," I say and quickly tug her pants and panties completely off. We make eye contact and she slowly spreads herself open to me. I'm not really in control, we're only pretending that I am. I run my tongue up one thigh and barely brush her core on my way over to her other thigh. She smells wet and ready. "Open yourself for me," I say. Her eyebrow arches and the corner of her mouth hitches up, not quite a smile, but enough of one to let me know she approves. She slowly reaches down and spreads herself open, her pussy glistening with need. I spread my tongue wide and lick her from the bottom of her slit all the way up to her clit. She moans appreciatively. I lick the soft flesh between her fingertips, and slip my tongue inside of her, tasting the tanginess of her arousal. "Touch yourself for me," I say. She slides her fingertip inside, gathering a bead of moisture to rub on her clit. Watching her spread open and masturbating for me is the ultimate turn on. I want to touch her, I want to touch myself, but this is too fascinating to interrupt. She thrusts her hips upward several times and I moan because I know what she is feeling. "Don't come yet." Her fingers stop immediately. Her breath is ragged and her thighs are quivering. She was closer than I thought.

"Please let me come for you," she says. I close my eyes and try hard not to shake at her request.

"No. Not yet," I quickly add after seeing the flash of almost anger in her eyes. "I will tell you when you can come." I kneel again between her legs, but this time I only use my hands. "Hold yourself open again." I slowly slip my index finger inside of her, marveling at the smoothness and tightness. Her slick walls squeeze me and contract the farther I slip into her.

"More," she says. I slide two fingers into her and she moans with appreciation. I'm desperate to please her, eager to make her come, but I keep my needs in check and build her up slowly, knowing that when she comes, it will be fierce. "Yes, just like that." Her face heats up and her teeth clamp down as she fights to breathe quietly. I lean forward and suck her clit into my mouth. She cries out and moves her whole body into me. I know that I can't stop her, I can only intensify it for her. She grabs the back of my neck and holds me in place as I devour her and my fingers twist inside of her. "Don't stop, Grace. Don't stop," she says. Her hips lift up to press against my mouth. Her orgasm rocks through her entire body as she rides every wave completely, her shouts of release echoing through the night. My body is humming and brimming right on the edge of my own orgasm just from watching hers. I put my head in her lap as we both try to calm down. She rests her hands on my shoulders, her fingertips absently stroking my skin. I gently pull out of her and wrap my arms behind her waist. We stay like that, close, quiet, complete. "I have no words," she says.

"You don't need any," I say. She motions for me to climb up on her, so on shaky legs, I stand and straddle her lap. She stares into my eyes for a long time.

I know at this moment, with our bodies as close as they can be, that I have fallen for her. She is everything I need, everything I want, and I know I have given her my heart without my own permission. I did exactly what I didn't want to do. I fell in love. Not just love, not even love with lust, but a place where my heart is free falling, constantly tumbling, falling deeper and deeper into an unknown abyss. I'm scared. I don't know when it ends, if it ends, or if I will crash and burn at the bottom. I'm afraid that she will see my untamed emotions when I look into her eyes so I avoid eye contact and focus instead on memorizing everything about her. How smooth her skin is, how beautiful she is, and how wonderful she feels in my arms. Finally she brings me to her for a kiss. It's a serious one and it couldn't be any more perfect. Her lips are soft, yet demanding, and I moan when she sucks my bottom lip into her mouth. Again, she is not gentle. She is possessive of me and I love every single moment of it. Of her. Of us. Her hands slide up the outside of my thighs to grab my waist and hold me in place. She gently lifts her hips into mine and I gasp as her mound presses into me.

"I need these off," she says, breaking our kiss to tug on my pants. I don't want to leave her body even for a moment, but the need to come is too great. I'm off of her lap and back on it in moments. "I missed you," she says. I was literally off her lap and back on it within seven seconds. My smile is shaky and tears threaten to spill out of the corners of my eyes. I close them and allow her touch to consume me and allow the physical need of the moment to push past the seriousness in my heart. I groan the moment I feel her fingertips graze my swollen, wet slit. I know I'm not going to last long. "Look at how wet you are," she says. I want to be embarrassed, but I'm empowered by how excited she is by it.

"Dripping," I say right before I lean down to kiss her. She slides two fingers into me and moves in and out until my hips automatically take over. Her other hand is on my neck keeping me close to her and close to her hand. Our lips are an inch apart, but we are no longer kissing. Now we are looking at one another. "Harder." I cry out as her fingers push into me as far and as fast as she can move them. There is no build up. There is only an instant, glorious explosion. I ride it out forever. It's the longest, most intense orgasm I've ever had.

"Wow." She brushes my hair out of my face. I can barely breathe. I just want to collapse into her and go to sleep. "Are you okay?" I can only nod. She holds me close to her and I wait until all of the aftershocks subside.

"That was…yeah, I have no words either." She wraps the blanket around me, around us, after I adjust my position and we sit there, holding one another for a very long, quiet time.

"Babe, wake up." I open my eyes and stare into Kerry's. "Let's go downstairs and get into bed. Then we can stretch out and I can hold you the right way." I lie there for a minute longer, enjoying her fingertips stroking my face. I nod and gently untangle myself from her. My back is sore because lawn furniture isn't designed for napping or fast and hard sex. I look around one last time before we head downstairs.

"Definitely my favorite place," I say.

"Mine, too. Well, here and the cliff," she says. I smile at the memory, too.

"If we have time tomorrow, I'd like to see it before we head to the airport," I say.

"We will make time."

Chapter Seventeen

Thankfully, the day is sunny and dry. My flight is at three, but I need to get to the airport by one because of the international guidelines. Kerry sneaked out early and came back with breakfast. We ate in bed and even shared some with Abram. Saying good-bye to him brought tears to my eyes. He's such a lover and I'm going to miss him terribly.

"You'll take care of him, right?" I ask. She kisses me swiftly.

"I promise. Now, let's go." She grabs my bag as I do a quick walk-through of the apartment. I quietly thank my aunt for her extreme kindness and tell her that I hope she and Kate are together now and happy. Tears sting my eyes again. I can't believe how emotional I am even though I've only been here a few weeks. I close the door behind me and follow Kerry downstairs. Leigh and Conor are waiting for me. A few tears escape when I hug them. They promise me that everything will be fine and wish me well. That makes me cry more.

"I don't know why I'm so emotional today." I climb into the passenger seat and take a deep breath. "This has been such a great trip. Except for the first few days, I've thoroughly enjoyed myself. Everybody here is so nice and supportive. I feel like I got to know Aunt Nola better than anybody else in the family had the chance to." Kerry reaches out and holds my hand for a minute. "And I met you." She brings my hand up to her mouth and places a soft kiss on the back of it.

"I was a jerk at the beginning, but I think you've forgiven me, right?" she says and we both giggle. I've forgiven her at least a dozen times already. Since we don't have her motorcycle and her car can only get us so far, we have to walk a ways to get to her favorite spot. It takes us a solid fifteen minutes, but well worth it in the end. The view is spectacular. We sit down and quietly look out across the sea.

"This is such a beautiful place. It's too bad you can't have your farm here," I say.

"Cliffs really aren't great for the animals. They don't know when to stop walking," she says. Good point. I've noticed that a lot of the farms don't have fences. Just two days ago we had to stop and wait for sheep to cross the road. Nobody thought it was a big deal.

"So how do you know which animals are yours and which belong to your neighbors? I mean, you don't have a lot of fences, especially by the road, so I'm sure the animals get mixed up," I say.

"They all have markings. Nobody is dumb enough to try to steal your sheep," she says.

"Really? Like ever in the history of Ireland, nobody has taken another person's property? You can't expect me to believe that."

She laughs. "You think too much, Grace. I'm just messing with you. Yes, there are fences, but most of them are stone or wood. Wire will hurt the animals. The property I'm looking at has stone walls. They aren't very high, but most sheep don't wander far from home."

"I'd like to come back and see your farm," I say. She looks at me for a long time before she nods. "Unless you don't want me to."

"Of course I want you to. I just know how busy you are. Plus, who knows when the shop will sell and when I will actually have the farm."

"Can we just pretend then?" I sound desperate. I grasp at anything to try to keep this fairytale alive. I know that Kerry is visiting me in a month, but we are both uncertain as to what happens after that. Long distance relationships don't last at all and she is entirely too beautiful and passionate to be alone. It's not fair and I know it. She reaches down and plucks a flower and hands it to me.

"A forget-me-not. Thank you for a fantastic time. I hope that you will always cherish your memories of Ireland and that you never forget me." She leans over and softly, yet deeply kisses me. She takes my breath away. When we finally break apart, I feel the tears spring up and I swallow hard. I don't want to cry. Not now. Not in front of her. She runs her fingertips across my cheek and the tears start flowing. She pulls me into her arms and holds me until I'm done.

"It's impossible for me to forget you. You're perfect." I sniff.

"Don't cry. There's nothing to cry about. We're amazing together and I'm going to see you soon, okay?" She cups my face and stares into my eyes. I believe her. I believe anything she says.

"I know. It's just hard to leave you and all of this." I'm actually dreading going home.

"Well, keep this flower and whenever you miss me, just look at it and think about our wonderful time together and that I will be with you again soon," she says. I want to cry again, but I keep it together. She puts her arm around me and holds me close. I don't want to leave her. I don't want to leave this beautiful place, or Abram, or The Irish Garden. I don't want to go back to my life. My boring, work drenched six-days-a-week job. I hold the flower close to my heart and kiss her. I know we have to go. I know it's time to head to the airport. She pulls me up to her and holds me and kisses my temple several times before she lets me go. We walk back to the car in silence. I have never known my heart to be this heavy before.

"At least the weather is nice for your flight out," she says. I think about Ailis, the kind, older lady who sat next to me on my flight over and how she told me the flights to Ireland are usually pretty rocky.

"I'm not the greatest flyer," I say.

"Neither am I. The longest flight I've ever been on was about four hours," Kerry says. She's going to hate me by the time she reaches Dallas. At least her layover is in Philadelphia so the longest leg of her journey to me is the six hours it takes to get there.

"Then you will hate me after your flight over to me. It's a bear," I say.

"I'm not worried. I can read or watch movies. As a real estate agent, you end up spending a lot of time alone. I know how to entertain myself." She smiles encouragingly at me. I know she's trying to help get my mind off of leaving, but it's hard when I know I won't be able to reach out for her whenever I want. Apparently, I'm not good at long distance or whirlwind affairs. I honestly don't know how Morgan does it. How can she even think of sharing herself with several women at once?

"Too bad there is this thing called the Atlantic Ocean between us," I say. Naturally, we reach the airport in record time without even trying.

"Isn't this how it always is? When you are in a hurry, everybody is in your way. When you have all the time in the world, there is nothing in your way," she says. She surprises me by parking in the garage instead of just dropping me off at the curb.

"What are you doing?" I ask.

"I'm not going to just drop you off. I'm going to make sure you get to your gate and that we have a few minutes together that aren't side by side in a car." She makes me smile. I reach for the door handle when she parks, but she pulls me back to her. "Close your door." I shiver. She's doing that control thing again. It's my weakness. She cups my face in her hands and gives me the longest, deepest kiss. My heart is in my throat and I moan with appreciation. I'm desperate for more. I clutch her to me. I don't care that people can see us. After several intense minutes, we break apart. I rub my thumb on her bottom lip.

"Now that's what I call a send-off," I say. She gives me her crooked, sexy smile. My heart jumps. I sigh and reluctantly get out of the car. My legs are wobbly and it takes me a few seconds to steady myself.

"Are you all right?" she asks. She takes my bag from me and reaches for my hand.

"When you kiss me like that, I can't quite function right away," I confess. She grabs my free hand and walks me into the airport. The airport is huge, but Kerry knows exactly where to go and gets me to the security line, again, in no time. She pulls me to the side into a semi-private alcove before the line starts.

"Listen, don't be sad that you're leaving. I'll see you in just a few short weeks, okay?" She cups my chin to make sure that I don't look away. Her strength gives me strength.

"I know. I'm fine now. I've always hated good-byes."

"They certainly aren't fun. Please let me know when you've made it home safely, okay?" I love that she hasn't stopped touching me. Her fingers tuck my hair behind my ear and run along my jawline. "Favorite part about Ireland?"

"You," I say and kiss her softly. I feel her moan into me as we deepen the kiss. I hear giggling off in the distance and pull away from her. "Okay, I have to go. I will talk to you soon, okay?"

"Be careful and good luck," she says. I grab my bags and make my way through security. She waits until I'm through and am able to wave to her one last time. I could stare at her for hours. As slight as she is, she commands attention. I'm aware of other people noticing her, too, and smile because she is mine, at least for a little while longer.

CHAPTER EIGHTEEN

Hey, Earth to Grace." Morgan snaps her fingers in front of me, trying to bring me back to our meeting about the Beck account. Alisa gathered great information at the meeting earlier in the week, and Morgan and her staff are trying to convince me to sign off on their idea.

"Oh, sorry, guys. Can you give me a few minutes?" I ask. Morgan dismisses them for a fifteen minute break. She asks the last one who leaves to close the door on her way out. I'm either in trouble because I'm not participating, or she's mad as hell because I'm not concentrating. Either way, I'm about ready to have my ass handed to me.

"Grace, I know this has been a hard week getting back into the swing of things, but I really need you to focus. This isn't just about you. These people, this company, we all need your input to knock this thing out of the park. Okay?" I stare at her and try hard to shake Kerry from my thoughts, but she's nestled deep inside of me and isn't going anywhere soon. "Just give me ten minutes. That's all I want. Then you can go back to your office and pine away for Kerry." I bristle because she says it to me in a condescending way. I take a deep breath before I answer.

"I know, I know. You've been covering for me since I left and I owe you so much. Okay, let me review the boards again real quick and I'll tell you what I think."

She heads over to the coffee maker and pours herself a cup, giving me my requested space and time. I'm not excited about their idea. It's hard to make gardening tools sexy and exciting, and her group barely tried.

"Your client caters to the middle class, but all of these suggestions are geared toward the one percent. Those people don't even know a shovel from a hoe. They have gardeners and arborists to take care of their properties. And based on what Alisa said about Beck, he's very grounded. You need to think dads who work during the week and need tools to help them finish their yard projects in record time so they can spend time playing with their families after work and on the weekends."

"That's been done though," she says. I know her feelings are hurt, but this is what we do best. We tell each other the truth and produce better material because of it.

"Yeah, so the challenge is to make it special. Make it current. Find out his boundaries. What does he stand for?"

Morgan stares at me for a few seconds, processing what I've said. "This is why I need you here. I need that brain power."

"Maybe he has a gay brother and he's okay with a commercial of two dads working the yard, then playing football or wrestling with their kids and dog after the lawn is mowed. Or if he's not into that, show a family who fosters dogs on the weekends who keep their yard cleaned up to protect and nurture the animals. Just something more people can relate to and apply it to their lives. This stuff? You can do better." I point to the presentation spread out on the conference room table.

She sighs. "You're right. Well, can we get on a conference call with Beck later this morning? You are so much better at schmoozing with the clients." I agree to that. "Thanks, Grace. I'll set it up with Beck's admin and I'll let you know." I jot down a few notes so that I don't forget them because even I know I've only given about twenty-five percent this week since I've been back. "Any word yet on the shop? Any potential buyers?"

"Nothing yet, but it's still early. They're posting it under both residential and commercial. From what I understand, their zoning laws are almost non-existent. That would be a kick ass house if somebody wanted to convert it. Fantastic location. I'm sorry you weren't able to see it."

"Your relationship with Kerry might have been different if I was there," she says.

"Probably, but our chemistry is unmistakable. We would have hooked up, but maybe only once or twice." I know Morgan is watching me, so I try to look uninterested in this conversation even though my palms are sweaty and I keep trying to swallow my heart. I refuse to reach for my water because then she will see my hands shake.

"Have you talked to her a lot since you've been back?" I know what she's doing. We've been friends long enough.

I shrug. "A few times. She's excited about coming to Dallas. There is so much she wants to see." Mostly me, but I leave that part out.

"Don't play with me, woman. I know that look. That lost puppy dog look with the sad eyes. You're in love with her," she says.

I jerk my head up. I was not expecting that. "No, I'm not," I say defensively.

"Yes, you are. I've seen you this way twice before. In college with Julie and this last one." She still won't say her name. "You were just like this, only now you're worse." I shake my head and she stops me. "Yeah, you've got it bad. I can't wait to meet her." She rubs her hands together and I shake my head at her again.

"I just didn't like how fast everything went. I was there, we had a great time together and had really, really good sex, and then it was time to come home. I'm completely lost. We didn't have time for any afterglow really," I say. Morgan looks at me like I'm crazy. "You know, the time when you have really great sex and then cuddle and snuggle and lock yourselves in a room for weeks until one of you has to work or eat."

"That's not true. That's what you did the final week there," Morgan says. She does have a point. Kerry and I stayed in the apartment for two days straight, naked and hungry for one another.

"Okay, then maybe it's because I wanted more and had to come home. We're still in the getting to know one another phase so I wasn't done getting to know her."

"I promise not to bother you girls when she gets into town next week. At least not on days when you have something planned."

"Because you know I will kill you if you bother me. I'm half tempted to ask for my key back from you just in case you decide to do something embarrassingly stupid." I narrow my eyes threateningly.

She holds her hands up in a surrendering gesture. "I wouldn't think about it. I know how important she is to you and wouldn't dream of interrupting." She smiles. "I'm happy for you, Grace. Now, get out of here so I can yell at my team. I'll call you when I hear back from Beck." We don't hug at work because we want everyone to think our relationship is work only, so when I walk by her to get out of the room, I wink at her and am rewarded with a hefty smack on my ass. So much for professionalism.

❖

"Grace. I don't want you to get into trouble at work." Kerry and I are Skyping. I'm getting ready for bed and she's just waking up. Technically, I woke her up, but she assures me she was planning on getting up early today. She looks delicious. I wish I was curled up next to her, our bodies entwined.

"It's not a problem. Really. It's just a funny story. I'd say get out of my head, but I kind of like you there," I say. I'm rewarded with a smirk. "How's Abram doing?"

"He's fine. I think he misses you. He's forever looking out of the window, according to Leigh. She came by to see Emma and

Ian and filled me in on what's happening at the shop. They are staying away from the wedding business in case the shop sells before the orders can be filled, but are getting a lot of flowers for spring parties, dances, graduations, and things like that."

"Any nibbles on the business?" I ask. It's not something I want to really talk about, but we do need to discuss it.

"A few people have called, but I've not set up any appointments. I don't expect it to be a long wait though. I just hope it stays local and a giant business doesn't buy it. I don't expect that to happen, but you never know."

Her answer depresses me. "I'm sure it won't be long and I have last say on who buys it anyway, right? I mean, I don't have to accept the offers if I don't approve?"

"No, you don't, but you also don't want to miss an opportunity. The market is okay, but not great. I say if somebody has the money, then sell it. Don't worry about what I think." Sure, like I'm heartless.

"Well, we can talk about it when we do get an offer. In the meantime, let's talk about you and the fact that you are going to be here this week. I'm so excited. It's already hot here, so don't worry about sweaters or jackets. As a matter of fact, you don't have to worry about clothes at all if you don't want to," I say. She smiles at me.

"I will pack light, I'm sure. I want to have plenty of room for baby clothes and toys for Ian." I've told her that I already have a stack of cute clothes that I couldn't resist buying. She is going to be one hundred times worse. I've scheduled one afternoon where we shop, but not a lot of other things. I plan to utilize every minute reacquainting myself with her body.

"Go to bed, sweets. It's late there and I don't want you to get in trouble at work anymore because of me. Please get some sleep. I will call you Thursday before I board the plane, okay?" I nod like it's not a big deal that she will be here in three days. It takes us awhile to say our good-byes and even then I'm reluctant to hang up. My condo is ready for her. I've scrubbed and cleaned everything twice already. I will go grocery shopping Wednesday after work and stock the refrigerator with everything. I don't want to have to leave unless it's an agreed upon outing. I put away my laptop and turn my alarm on. I have to get up in five hours and put in extra time this week since I'm taking Friday and Monday off. Sherry wasn't excited, but she really can't complain too much about time I want off. I have fifty days of vacation left, even after taking time off for Ireland. It's just a matter of time before they reevaluate the company's vacation policy, mostly because of me. Tomorrow morning, I have another meeting with Morgan and her team, and another meeting in the afternoon with our post-production team. The Beck account will be presented Wednesday and Morgan asked that I stand in with them. All of these are important business matters and I find my interest waning. My job seems so superficial and empty since I've been back. I can't seem to get interested in it. I'm surviving strictly by the mechanics of it. My heart is somewhere else.

Chapter Nineteen

The first thing I do, before I even kiss her or hug her is touch her face. I can't believe she is right here in front of me. She clutches me, but she understands my need to look at her before we embrace.

"You made it," I say right before I kiss her soundly on the mouth in front of everybody at the airport. She holds me close. We're in everybody's way, but nobody says anything to us.

"I'm finally here. What a journey," she says. I grab one of her bags and her hand and take her away from everybody. She is surprised at the size of the airport.

"Tell me all about your trip," I say as I slip into the driver's seat of my SUV. I watch as she runs her hands on the leather and touches everything within reach.

"This is a very nice car. And it's so big," she says. I instantly feel a mixture of pride and guilt. "Okay, the trip wasn't as bad as I thought it would be. I read some, watched a movie, thought about us."

I lean over and kiss her. "I'm so happy."

"Take me to your home," she says. I pull out into traffic and try not to watch her face as she processes the size of the city, the traffic, and the overall environment. We are just getting into rush hour traffic and I know it's just going to get worse. At least my condo isn't far from downtown so we will be driving against most of the traffic. "The buildings are so big and bright. And it's so sunny." I hand her an extra pair of sunglasses that she gratefully slips on. We reach my condo in thirty minutes. I decide we're going to stay hidden the rest of the night. We kiss again in the elevator, our passion instantly igniting. By the time we reach my door, my shirt is already untucked and Kerry's blouse is halfway unbuttoned. I barely turn the doorknob before she is flat up against me, pulling me to her. "I've missed you so much." Kerry pushes me up against the door, her mouth all over me in an instant.

"I've missed you, too, so much. And this. I've missed your mouth…" The rest of the sentence is a moan as she pushes my bra up and roughly licks my nipple. I'm completely at her mercy and weak with need. She unbuttons my shirt and reaches around to unhook my bra. I unzip my pants and kick them off. I'm standing in front of her in a red lace thong. She drops to her knees in front of me.

"You're so beautiful," she says as she runs her hands up my thighs, over my panties, and across my bare stomach. I close my eyes and enjoy. When her hands reach up and cup my breasts, I put my hands over hers and squeeze. I'm rewarded with a moan. She leans forward and kisses my stomach, running her tongue on the outer edge of my thong. I lean my shoulders back against the door so that I can thrust my mound closer to her mouth. She grabs my hips and holds me steady. "Where is your room?"

"Behind you on the left," I say. She stands and pulls me into her arms. She knows how much I love to be naked when she's dressed. How the friction of her clothes drives me crazy. We kiss the entire way back to my room while I diligently remove her clothes. She is thinner than before, but just as beautiful. We eagerly get to know one another again, the three weeks since our last visit seems like a lifetime ago.

❖

"Are you hungry? Tired?" I ask. She's on her side facing me, her hand holding mine. It's already after nine o'clock and I know she has to be one or the other or both. She closes her eyes and drops back on the pillow.

"I'm running on fumes," she says.

I jump up. "I'm so sorry. Let me grab some snacks. I'll be right back," I say. I hit the kitchen and grab fruit, cheese, and crackers. I bounce on the bed as she scoots over. "I noticed you've lost weight." I point to the tray. "Eat."

"I love it when you're bossy," she says. We smile at one another. The last time I was bossy, we had an explosive night.

"I've really missed you. I've missed us," I say. Kerry kisses me, softy and deeply. I sigh and melt into her. "You need to eat and get some sleep. Jet lag is awful." We finish our picnic after she insists that she's had enough food. I promise her a big breakfast in the morning and order her to sleep. She reaches out to me. I slide into her arms. Even though I'm not tired yet, I lie and enjoy her warmth and the fact that she is in my arms again.

Chapter Twenty

I can't believe there are so many people here just wanting breakfast. And on a weekday. Aren't most people working?" Kerry asks. We're sitting at the little breakfast nook down the street and there's a thirty minute wait. Thankfully, we have enough to talk about and full coffee cups.

"I promise you, it's so worth it," I say. She surprises me by kissing me in front of everybody waiting. Some people smile at us while others look away. I think it's great that it's not even a concern for her.

The older couple sitting next to us strikes up a conversation after hearing Kerry's accent. They, too, are immediately taken with her charm. When the restaurant calls the couple's name, they invite us to dine with them. Kerry thanks them, but declines after explaining that we haven't seen one another in almost a month and we need quality time together.

"Even when you turn people down, they still love you." She laughs. "Yep, you're going to do well here. All that Irish charm," I say. I've already noticed a lot of people staring at her. Last night, after a five hour power nap, she woke me up the way I want to wake up every morning, spread wide with her warm mouth all over me. It was a delightful surprise to say the least. This extended weekend will be sprinkled with short and long naps, meals in bed, and her in control of me during all waking hours.

"How was work this week?" she asks. I love that even though she's curiously looking around at the restaurant and the people, when she talks to me, her eyes are always focused on mine.

"Well, I didn't get scolded anymore," I say.

"I can't wait to meet Morgan and see what she's like," Kerry says. After breakfast, we're going to my office so that she can see where I work. Morgan has invited us to her party on Saturday night. It's an open invitation. I wouldn't commit us because I don't know what we're going to be doing Saturday.

"Please don't hurt her," I say. "She needed to kick my ass because my head was still in Ireland with you." She kisses me again.

"Since when have you known me to lose my temper?" Her angelic look is endearing, but doesn't fool me.

"Never. Not you, you sweet Irish lassie," I say with my best Irish accent.

"Very nice. You're an excellent student." She lifts her eyebrow. I shiver knowing full well what she means.

"I have the best teacher." Here, in the middle of this busy restaurant, I want her. She can turn me on with just a look, a soft touch, a word. Thankfully, or not, we're called to be seated. I take a deep breath and follow the hostess to a table by the window so we can see downtown. We review the menu while our waitress runs to get us fresh coffee. "If you have any questions, let me know. Everything here is delicious and I do expect you to eat well today." I settle for French toast, and Kerry orders an omelet with potatoes and toast.

"Satisfied?" she asks, referring to her order.

"Not yet."

That perks her interest. "Oh, really? I thought for sure you would be for at least a few more hours. We can eat fast and go home."

"Tempting, but I promised you a quick tour of my town and my work. Then we can stay sequestered for the rest of your time here." She nods.

After forty-five minutes of catching up on Howth and Dublin events and stories about the people I know there, I pay the check and we head over to my office. It's a beautiful day, not too hot yet, so we decide to walk the four blocks to Shumer & Bristol. Again she surprises me by holding my hand as if it's the most normal thing in the world. I'm not sure how she is going to be once we get to the office though. I've never brought my private life to work before so I'm sure this is going to get people gossiping. I find that I don't mind. I like my relationship with Kerry. I'm not embarrassed by it. She's beautiful, smart, and headstrong. I bet that most of my colleagues will be jealous after meeting her.

"Late start today, boss?" Billy, the building's security guard, razzes me a little. He's fierce, yet adorable, and always softens for me.

"I'm actually not on the clock today. Billy, this is Kerry. She's visiting me from Ireland." Billy strikes up a conversation about his recent trip to Ireland and Scotland. After five minutes, I interrupt only because I'm bored and selfish and want her back. She is nothing but kind to him and he, in turn, is smitten with her. "I love that you're very sweet to everybody. It's an endearing trait."

"He's completely taken with you, too. He just loves beautiful women," she says. We grab the elevator and take it up to the twenty-fourth floor. The doors open to hustle and bustle already in progress.

"Welcome to my hell." We dodge a few interns scurrying around. I wave hello to a couple people as we make our way around to the back where the executive offices are. I'm in jeans, boots, and a button-down linen shirt with my hair loose. Most employees probably don't recognize me. I'm never this casual.

"Grace, I thought you weren't coming in today." Alisa finds me immediately. "Oh, I'm sorry. Hi, I'm Alisa." She shakes Kerry's hand. Her smile is friendly and genuine. I introduce them and suddenly it clicks for Alisa. I almost see the lightbulb turn on.

"Oh, oh. Okay, um, we can talk about it next week. No worries."
She leaves in a hurry.

"Was it something I said?" Kerry asks.

"Yes, but nothing to worry about," I say. I lead her back to
my office and after introducing her to my assistant, Tina, I usher
her in and lock the door behind her. "Finally. I didn't think I
would ever get you up here."

She walks over to the floor to ceiling windows. "This is
a great office with a nice view. Buildings everywhere, people
everywhere. Why were you overwhelmed in Dublin? It's not
even close to this size."

"I'm not familiar with Dublin, but I've lived in Dallas for
the last eight years so it's what I'm used to." I walk up behind her
and put my arms around her waist and rest my forehead on her
shoulder. "I'm so happy you're here."

She turns in my embrace, lifts my chin toward her, and places
the sweetest kiss on my lips. "I've missed you, too. I know long
distance is hard." My heart stops and panic flutters in my chest.
She doesn't elaborate. Is she okay with long distance or not?
Before my full blown fear takes over, we hear a knock at the door.

"Just a minute." I unlock the door and am greeted by
Morgan's happy face. She pushes right past me and heads straight
for Kerry.

"Hi. I'm Morgan. I heard there was a beautiful redhead in the
building. I had to come meet the girl who stole Gracie's heart,"
she says. I kind of want to throat punch her right now. "Oh, my. I
can see why." She hugs Kerry hello. I'm still trying to calm down
over Kerry's long distance comment.

"Hello, Morgan. I've heard interesting things about you,"
Kerry says.

Morgan laughs. "Hopefully not all bad."

"No, quite good actually. Grace is very fond of you," she
says. I shoot Morgan a look not to say anything else revealing.
She apparently gets the hint.

"So what are you lovelies doing here?" Morgan asks.

"I wanted to show Kerry where I work since I spend most of my time here," I say.

"This office is very impressive with a great view. I don't know that I would go home every night. And it's so large." It is quite the office. I have three desks: one for everyday work, a conference desk for more intimate meetings, and a drafting table. I'm also one of the few people who has a private bathroom. It's not much, but enough. Kerry thinks it's because I'm important. I know it's because Sherry doesn't want me away from my office too long.

"When did you get in?" Morgan asks. She knows the answer to this, so I'm assuming she's asking only to stick around. I sigh and sit down on my couch. This could be a while. Surprisingly, they are getting along pretty well. Of course, they are only discussing niceties so I expect both to behave. "If you want something to do tomorrow night, you can always come to my party. It's not going to be wild and crazy. Just a few friends, some wine, some barbecue, and good music. Think about it. Okay, I'll leave you two lovebirds alone. It was nice to meet you, Kerry, and I hope to see you tomorrow." She gives Kerry another quick hug and winks at me, ignoring my death stare. My heart jumps into my throat when I see Kerry lock my door after Morgan leaves.

"Does this thing really work? Or is it for show?" she asks.

"Oh, the lock works." I'd ask why she wants to lock the door, but I think I already know the answer.

She walks over to me and sits down on the couch.

"What a comfortable couch you have here." She runs her fingers across the back of the couch. She reaches my neck and traces her fingertips softly across my skin. I close my eyes and tilt my head back to give her better access. She scoots closer and I feel her warm, soft lips press against my neck. One hand slips into the opening of my shirt to touch my shoulder, the other tilts my head closer to her. She kisses me softly, yet possessively and I yield. She guides me beneath her and presses herself between my legs. Her hips push into me and I lift up, greedy for friction. She slips her hand between us and rubs my clit through my clothes. I clutch her closer not wanting this to happen so quickly, but the excitement of being in my office, having her here with me is too much and I greet my orgasm quickly and quietly. "Well, that was faster than I expected," she says. She smiles at me and my face flushes with a mixture of embarrassment and desire.

"I needed you."

She answers me with a soft kiss. "Have you always been this sexual?" she asks quietly.

I'm confused by the question. "What do you mean?"

"Don't get me wrong, I love that you are, but have you noticed that we have sex a lot?"

"Is that a problem?"

"Are you kidding me? I love it. I didn't think there was anybody else out there like me." She kisses me again, erasing my doubts.

"We do have fantastic chemistry. It's just too bad that we're worlds apart."

She is quiet, but only for a few moments. "That just means we have a lot of time to make up for when we're together."

I nod. "I like that logic. It works for us." She kisses me again and pulls me back into a sitting position.

"I've wrinkled you." She smoothes out my wrinkled shirt.

"So worth it. And we weren't interrupted once."

"Does anybody know you are here besides Morgan and Alisa?"

"Are you kidding me right now? I show up with a knockout redhead and lock myself in my office with her and you think nobody noticed? I bet half my staff is on the other side of this door trying to hear what's going on in here." Kerry smiles because she thinks I'm kidding. I smile back because I know I'm not. She gets up from the couch and stretches her long body, working out a few kinks from being in a strained position for the last five minutes.

"I would seriously look out of my office at least two hours a day if I had this view," she says. I walk up behind her again and put my arms around her waist. I don't like to not touch her when she is this close to me. We won't have this luxury most days. I run my hands up her stomach and back down to her hips. Her body is so tight and hard. She surprises me by grabbing my hand and moving it to the apex of her thighs. I moan my approval and stroke her mound up and down, moving steadily and with purpose. "Do you think anybody can see us right now?" she asks. I stop only to unbutton her jeans and unzip her fly. She gasps when I slip my fingers down the front of her panties, her wet core swollen with need. I move closer so that I'm flush behind her, giving my hand more room. She reaches out to steady herself against the window and widens her stance.

"If they can see us, they are probably enjoying this as much as we are. You're so wet." I don't realize that I'm pushing my hips into her every time I dip my finger low in her folds. I focus on her clit and massage it, slowly at first, then faster with more pressure. I stop only to pull her jeans and panties down to her knees, surprised that she doesn't stop me. I have full access to her now and waste no time. From behind, I slip two fingers inside of her. Her moan is delicious and rather loud, but I don't care. She bends over more, pressing both of her palms against the window and pushing herself into my hand. I place my free hand on her hip to guide her into me. She rocks against me, fast and hard and I can feel her slick walls tighten against my fingers, her impending orgasm within reach. She comes hard, but quietly, gritting her teeth as each wave crests. I slow my movements as her body trembles and twitches, and stop when her hips still. We are both very quiet. I lean forward and slowly slip out of her. She turns to me, grabs my face, and kisses me breathlessly.

"Christ, Grace. That wasn't supposed to happen," she says.

"Are you kidding? Of course that was supposed to happen. My office will never be the same." I will never be the same, I think to myself. "You are incredible, Kerry. Simply the best thing." She kisses me again and pulls up her panties and jeans. She leans back against the window.

"I really hope these are privacy windows. If not, we just gave all of downtown Dallas quite the show," she says. She is still shaking so I hold her in my arms and we stand there for a moment while we collect ourselves. We are interrupted by a knock on the door.

"Go away," I say quietly. Kerry laughs. "I'm not here."

"Grace, Grace are you in there? I have a quick question for you." It's Sherry. Great. My office smells like sex and my boss is about to enter. Kerry runs for the little bathroom and I look for the hand sanitizer.

"Just a moment," I say. I straighten my shirt and unlock the door.

"I know you aren't supposed to be here, but I have a quick question about the pancake account." She walks in and heads for the conference table, spreading out boards and diagrams. I head to the table and try to look interested. Sherry stops when she hears the water running in my bathroom. "I'm sorry. I didn't know you had somebody in here." Kerry walks out looking refreshed and beautiful.

"Hello. I'm Kerry." She reaches her hand out to shake Sherry's.

"Oh, are you Grace's friend from Ireland?" Sherry asks. Face palm. I cringe at my boss. She's talking to Kerry like she's twelve. I shoot Kerry an apologetic look. She winks at me.

"Yes. Grace has talked about Dallas so much that I decided to come for a visit. I've never been to the United States before." My boss starts going on and on about things we should do while Kerry is here. Kerry is so patient and sweet and gives Sherry her undivided attention. I decide to focus on the account so that I can answer questions and we can all get out of my office.

"What don't you like about this?" I ask. I'm confused. The team did everything we discussed.

"Are you sure? Why do I get the feeling that we're missing something." We both stare at the boards until it finally hits me. She came here just to meet Kerry. She probably smells the sex in the room and is sticking around to either make me uncomfortable or learn more about her. Probably both as I watch her turn her attention back to Kerry, asking her questions about her stay and what fun things there are to do in Ireland. When Kerry tells her she is the sheep shearing champion of southern Ireland, I lose it. For a second, I actually believe her but then she winks at me and I bust out laughing.

"For Christ's sake, Sherry, it's not as if Ireland is ancient. They have the internet and running water. Kerry even drives a car," I say.

"Oh, the one you caused her to wreck?" Sherry asks.

"Ouch. Oh, and Kerry, Luke never ran my card."

"I know. I told him not to," Kerry says, shrugging her shoulders as if it's no big deal.

"That wasn't what we agreed upon," I say. Sherry can tell I'm starting to get upset and wisely makes an exit.

"Well, you ladies have a good time. Grace, I'll see you next week. We can discuss this then." She gathers up her paperwork and heads out, closing the door behind her.

"Are you serious right now? You know all of that was my fault. I told you I would pay for it. You should have had Luke use my card."

She comes over to me and puts her hands on my shoulders. "Grace, it was an accident. He fixed it almost for free. I told him not to run your card."

"I know you're saving every penny for your farm and I know every penny helps. Why won't you let me help you?" She senses my frustration and kisses me quickly.

"I have a big family. We help each other out. It's no big deal. Come on, let's go back to the condo or go shopping for Ian." My heart softens when she mentions his name.

"I owe you," I say.

She grabs my shirt and gently pulls me to her. "You owe me nothing, okay? It was my decision. It's over with and we are not going to talk about it again." She punctuates her decision with a kiss. It works. My anger slips away.

"You win. Let's get out of here. We have more important things to worry about."

We sneak out of the office with very little interference and head to the closest mall. I figure we might as well knock it out while we are out of the condo because I have a feeling once we are back there, it's going to take a lot for us to get back out again.

Chapter Twenty-one

"A re you sure you want to go?" Kerry and I are in bed, wrapped up in one another when she decides we should go to Morgan's party. I'm okay either way. If we stay here, I get her all to myself and if we go, I get to show her off to all of my friends. Win, win.

"I want to know everything about you. Yesterday, I got to hang out at your job and see you in action. Today, I get to see you hang out with your friends. This is why I'm here. To get to know you better and see where and how you live. Remember, I took you all around Ireland. I think it's only fair that you show me more about you." Guilt trip sold. I sigh and send Morgan a text that we will be there in a little bit. I toss the phone on the nightstand. Kerry pounces on me. "I promise to make it up to you." I nod like I don't believe her. She kisses me until I do.

After much negotiation on how long we are going to be gone and wardrobe advice, we finally head to Morgan's. The party is in full swing when we arrive.

"There you both are!" Morgan greets us with a group hug and drags us inside. She is already tipsy which surprises me. Normally, she doesn't like to lose control, especially in a roomful of lesbians. That never ends well. "Come in, come in. We have so many people here who want to meet the mysterious Irish woman who has…" I put my hand over her mouth and shake my head.

She laughs and pulls back. "We all want to meet you." She grabs Kerry's hand and drags her to the living room to introduce her around. At this point, I'm sure Kerry has to know she has my heart. Women don't do what we've done and share what we have without having strong feelings involved. I decide to grab a glass of wine instead of helicoptering Morgan. She's going to say what she's going to say whether I want her to or not. I can hear my friends squawk over Kerry and I watch the introduction from the doorway. Kerry is fantastic with new people. I watch every single one of my friends smile genuinely at her, knowing they, too, are fascinated by her. Morgan slips away from the crowd and stands beside me.

"She's fucking perfect. And I'm jealous. Don't let her slip away," Morgan says.

"Well, a Dublin-Dallas relationship really isn't in the cards for us. I have no idea what I'm going to do," I say.

"You make it work. Simple as that," she says, then leaves me. There is no way I would take Kerry away from her family, and I can't leave my life here. I guess we will ride this out until we drift apart. I convince myself I'm okay with that, but the thought actually terrifies me. A long weekend once a month isn't fair to either one of us. She's far too special to me to tether her like that. If I really care about her, I should do the honorable thing and stop this before it turns into something we both end up regretting. Kerry looks at me from across the room and raises an eyebrow at me. That's my cue. I head over to her and whisk her away from my inquisitive friends.

"She needs to have some genuine Texas barbecue, ladies. I'll bring her back in a few minutes." We head outside and I help Kerry fix her plate. She's unsure of what she should eat, so I advise her to try a little bit of everything. We find an empty bench and she dives into the food. She impresses me by cleaning her plate of everything but the baked beans. They are too sweet for her.

"If I lived here, I would gain five pounds every week. This is delicious," she says.

"Funny because I think the same about if I lived in Ireland. I would be huge."

"Well then, we'll just have to work out to stay fit and beautiful," she says. I toast to that. "Now, does Morgan have any local beer? I mean, I can get Bud Light in Dublin."

"Your wish is my command. Can I leave you alone or will I have to fight the lesbians off of you when I return?"

She shrugs. "Well, I'm yours so you don't have to worry. Although I did see a very cute butch girl in there I wouldn't mind..." My possessive kiss shuts her up. I leave her, both of us smiling, and head for the kitchen. By the time I return with a local beer from Deep Ellum Brewery, she is already flanked by two young lesbians. I roll my eyes. She stands up when I reach her because there isn't any place for me to sit now.

"Really? I was gone for like two minutes." I smile so she knows I'm teasing. Right there, in front of her new friends and everybody watching us, she pulls me into her arms and kisses me. Not a cute peck on the lips kind of kiss, but the kind that makes everything around you disappear. The kind that makes people around you blush and swoon. "Okay, you're forgiven," I say, breathlessly and unashamed. I step out of her arms and hand her the beer, because if I don't leave her embrace, I will embarrass both of us by dropping to my knees. "This is from a local brewer. It's not as strong as an Irish Red, but similar." I watch as she takes a sip, the tiniest of bubbles resting against her lips as she pulls the bottle away from her mouth.

"Mmm. Not bad for American beer," she says. I pinch her side playfully. Two girls I used to play softball with, Lindsay and Ellie, come over and introduce themselves to Kerry. They draw us into conversation and we spend at least a half of an hour with them. Morgan eventually drags Kerry over to meet other friends.

"So what's the story there?" Lindsay asks.

"What do you mean?"

"She's from Ireland. Are you girls going to try the long distance thing or not? Because if you aren't, then I might want to start something with her. She's really great," she says. My mouth literally drops open. I can't even speak. Lindsay laughs and playfully pushes my shoulder. "You should see your face right now. I'm just kidding. But she is wonderful. You should hang onto her. You deserve this, Grace. It's been a long time for you." Even she won't mention my ex's name. That relationship was more toxic than I thought.

"Thanks, Lindsay. What's going on with you? Anything?" Lindsay is a very nice woman, but has very little self-confidence and tends to date the wrong girls, too.

"Nah. It's okay though. I'm not ready to settle down yet. I'm only twenty-five. I have plenty of time," she says. I see her watching Morgan out of the corner of her eye and automatically think of playing matchmaker. Morgan wants stability. Lindsay needs somebody to boost her confidence and Morgan just might be that person. I'd casually bring it up to her today, but she's not in the right frame of mind right now. Plus, she's flitting about, my girlfriend on her arm, so I file it away for next week instead. After about twenty minutes of having friends come up to tell me how happy they are for me, I decide it's time to go home and celebrate how happy everybody is for us. Kerry is sitting with Morgan and a few others.

"Have you had enough of my friends? Can we go home yet?" I whisper. Kerry leans up and cups my face closer to her ear to hear me better. "I miss you." She faces me and kisses my lips.

"Ladies, thank you so much for your hospitality and kindness. It's been a pleasure getting to know you," she says. My friends protest a bit, but Morgan shuts them down and gets us to the door quickly.

"I want you to stay, but I know that your time is limited. Go have fun. Kerry, you're wonderful. Be good to Gracie." Morgan kisses us and shoves us out of the door.

"Trust me. That was the best thing Morgan could have done for us," I say. Kerry still looks surprised. "We can always go back." I turn and head back to the door. Kerry grabs me.

"I trust you. Let's go home," she says, kissing me hard. She makes me smile.

CHAPTER TWENTY-TWO

Sunday we are blessed with much needed rain. Our outdoor plans are scratched and we decide to stay inside. I offer to take her to the Dallas Museum of Art, but she assures me she just wants to relax. I'm sure it's jet lag, or the fact that we've had sex every waking moment, but she is exhausted. I let her drift back to sleep and head to the kitchen to make us breakfast. I have all of the ingredients for a bacon, egg, and potato casserole. It will take about an hour to prepare and cook. I slip it in the oven and head to the bathroom for a much needed shower. I'm deliciously sore everywhere and smile the entire time I scrub down. I'm genuinely happy. Kerry is wonderful. This is great and bad at the same time. I'm going to miss her when she leaves tomorrow. I'm already thinking about my next trip to Ireland. And logically I know to cut this off right now. Let this just be what this is. An in the moment affair. But I can't. My heart is already heavily invested. The one thing I wasn't going to allow to happen. I was going to keep my heart out of this. Too late.

"Babe, are you hungry?" I lean down and place a soft kiss on Kerry's cheek. She stirs and makes a small nondescript noise. I feel guilty for waking her up, but I know she needs to eat. I nuzzle her cheek and her ear until she opens her eyes. "I made you breakfast in bed. Do you need to sleep more or can you eat?"

"I'm surprisingly hungry." She moves into a sitting position. "Thank you, love, this looks great." I automatically lift my eyebrows when she calls me love and there is a slight hesitation in her movements when she sees my reaction. This breakfast just got interesting. I play it off and move over to the other side of the bed to eat next to her. We both devour our breakfast, obviously needing energy.

"We can watch a movie if you want. What kind of movies do you like?" I ask.

"I watch every single movie that I can. Remember, I'm twenty-eight years old and still live at home. I need to escape every night."

"Stop. You live at home because you are saving up for something better. There's nothing wrong with that. Plus, that's just the way it is over in Ireland. I admire what you're doing. It's smart. Things are just different over here," I say.

"It's embarrassing. I didn't want to tell your friends that I still live at home. I wanted to impress them for you," she says.

I laugh. Probably not the best timing because I see hurt flash in her eyes and I quickly explain. "I'm only laughing because every single woman at that party would jump at the opportunity to have you move in with them. One of my friends actually asked me if we were going to do the long distance thing, and if not, could she step in. A woman living at home at your age is not a weakness. Sure, if you weren't saving up your money and playing video games and smoking weed living in your parents' basement then yeah, that's kind of a loser life, but you have goals and dreams. It's admirable."

"I just sometimes feel like I'm not good enough for you. You have this incredible job. You live in a great condo in one of the best cities in the world. Your car is beautiful, your office is fantastic. You have the perfect life," she says.

"That's so not true. I work too hard, too many hours when I should be focusing on myself. I finally find the girl of my dreams and she lives four thousand miles away. My car? It's just a thing. My office? Designed to keep me there late every night. My life isn't perfect. I struggle every day with my decisions. We all do. This is normal," I say.

"The girl of your dreams, huh?"

That makes me smile. "Without a doubt. Sure, she was stubborn and mean when I first met her, but I broke her down and now she's mine," I say, right before she jumps on me and tickles me.

"Stubborn and mean? Take it back," she says. I shake my head no. She tickles me some more. "Take it back." I smile at her and shake my head again.

"Stubborn. And. Mean." I over pronounce each word. She growls at me and slides my hands up over my head. Her body is already on top of mine, but now I can't move at all. "Stubborn." She barely runs her lips over mine and pulls back when I lean in for a kiss. "And." She moves her lips down to my neck. I feel her warm breath against my skin, but I know she isn't going to kiss me. Her featherlike kisses are driving me crazy, but I keep going. "Mean." She leans up to look in my eyes.

"Do you really think that?" She releases my hands, and I automatically reach out to hold her face close to mine.

"Oh, God, no. I'm just having fun. Yes, you are stubborn, but never mean. Truly. The girl of my dreams."

"Grace, what are we going to do? We both know long distance relationships never last."

"We take this day by day. Hour by hour if we have to. Let's not make any decisions right now, okay? I have you for another twenty-four hours and I'd like to enjoy every single minute of them. Can we do that? Please?" I'm actually begging her. She nods. I pull her to me and we stay like that for a long time. I'm wondering what is going to happen when she leaves and I can only imagine that she is doing the same.

"Am I hurting you?" Her body is more to my side than actually on top of me and her weight feels great. She fits me perfectly.

"You could never hurt me. You are too slight." I quickly add that part because emotionally she could destroy me.

"But I'm taller than you, and certainly stronger," she says.

"You are perfect." I'm suddenly very sad because this is true and I don't know how many more of these moments we will have.

❖

"My bag is packed," Kerry says.

"You mean bags, right?" I ask. She has three sitting by the door.

"Well, those two are for Ian. Mine is packed." Her flight is at eleven tomorrow morning, which means we need to leave at eight. That gives us ten hours to sleep and have our last few hours of alone time. We haven't discussed the future. I have no idea if I will see her again. I know I want to and I know I will do everything I can to get me there or her here, but I don't know how she feels.

"That baby is a month old and already spoiled," I say.

"He's a Mulligan and he deserves it. Plus, he's the cutest baby in the world and I can't wait to see him again," she says. I love how much her face lights up when she mentions him. She will make a great mom someday. I set the alarm for six thirty and reach out to her. She slides into the bed with me and rests against me.

"Thanks for coming all this way to see me and get to know my life."

"Dallas is large. You have a great life here. I'm kind of jealous," she says.

"My life is nothing to be jealous of, trust me. I work too hard and I do nothing but work."

"You have nice things, a nice home, and for the most part, nice friends," she says. She told me last night that a few of the women at the party were snobby, which doesn't surprise me. Morgan really is my only true friend.

"I'm sorry a few were rude to you. Some women just have a hard time around a beautiful woman. Most of those girls I only see during softball season. I miss half the games so I'm not super close with them," I say. "But I'm most sorry that we didn't get out more. Wait. No, no I'm not sorry. I love our alone time." She holds my hand.

"I did have a great time. Texas is so very different from Ireland. And the weather here? It's so hot. We should have gone swimming." Last night I took her up to the roof where there is a community pool for our building. We almost skinny dipped, but at the last moment, a group of people showed up. By the time we got back to the condo to put on swimsuits, we were so turned on that swimming was completely forgotten.

"I liked what we did instead."

She kisses my cheek. "So did I."

"So, what happens now? What do we do?"

She sighs heavily. "I honestly don't know. I want to see you, but I don't expect you to come over all of the time and I can't afford to fly back here much. I just don't have the money. It's not fair to you or me." This sounds like her mind is made up. I feel my heart speed up and crash into reality, a thousand pieces scatter inside of me. I'm still. I don't even know what to say. I lift her chin up so that her eyes meet mine. She is somber and there are tears in her eyes. I know I can't talk right now, so I communicate the only way I can. I lean down and kiss her softly. I put everything I can into that gentle kiss. She clutches me almost desperately. I know in my heart that tonight will be our last night together. I slide down so that we are facing one another. She whimpers and I know she is trying not to cry.

"Shh. It's okay." I kiss away the tears that start falling. "It's okay." I can't stop saying that. I know that it's not okay, but if I say it enough times, then maybe I will even believe it. I touch her softly as if it's my first time, but with the realization that this is the last. I want to try to memorize everything about her. Every curve, every scar, every freckle. I watch her slip out of her clothes, but my hands never leave her body. She helps me out of mine and pulls me to her the moment I'm completely naked. We aren't rushed even though time isn't on our side. I know that tonight will have to last me a lifetime. I move and settle between her legs, never breaking our kiss. She wraps her arms around my shoulders and raises her knees up so our bodies are touching everywhere. She fits me so well. I run my fingertips over her face and down to her soft neck. I feel her strong, pulsating heartbeat against my hand. I look at her and tell her how I feel without saying a word. Her heartbeat quickens. She knows. I spend the next several minutes kissing the softness above her collarbone, the slight valley between her breasts, the smooth skin of her stomach. I put my hand over her mound, feeling her heat on my fingertips, and run my tongue from one thigh to the other. Our passion is building, but it's different. Now we are connected with our hearts and we both know it. She pulls me back up to her.

"Stay with me," she says. Her vulnerability breaks my heart even more. I reach between our bodies and stroke her tenderly until her hips move against me. She is wet and ready and I slide one, then two fingers inside of her. She breaks our kiss to gasp. I watch her face as I steadily build her up. She surprises me by tilting me off of her so that I am beside her and we're facing one another.

"Are you okay?" I stop my movements.

"Don't stop. I just want to touch you, too." She runs her hands down my body and slips two fingers inside of me, knowing I'm ready for her. I moan deeply. No matter if I'm expecting her touch or not, feeling her inside of me takes my breath away. I catch up to her quickly and we move together, kissing, stroking, and building one another up. I listen to her heavy breathing against my mouth, moans escaping when I bring her closer. "Please, Grace." I know what she means. I focus on her touch and allow her to take me higher and higher. I'm ready.

"Now, Kerry, now." I break the kiss and watch her as her orgasm explodes. I've never seen anything more beautiful. She keeps eye contact with me as long as she can. Her body rocks against my hand, against my body, and a pink flush splashes across her skin. I come seconds after she does. I selfishly wanted to watch her, wanted to have that image in my head forever. When my orgasm overtakes me, I lean forward and place my head on her shoulder and cry out with a mixture of the pleasure of her touch and the pain of her leaving me.

CHAPTER TWENTY-THREE

This is bullshit. Have you talked to her at all?" Morgan is standing in front of my desk, her hands on her hips, waiting for my answer. "You've been moping all week. Just figure out a way to make this work."

"She called me last week to tell me she made it home safely." It physically hurt me to hear her voice. I clutched my heart the entire conversation, thankful she couldn't see me and how distraught I am over losing her. She was never mine to begin with. "Look, I just need to get through the sale of the business and then I can move on and we can do that thing we talked about. You know, settling down. And speaking of which, what do you think about sweet Lindsay?"

"Quit trying to change the subject. You are a hot mess right now. Look at you. Have you even eaten in a week? And you approved the worst commercial ever made. You've got to get your shit together, girl. Everything about you is suffering."

I put my head in my hands and groan. "I know, I know. I have no idea what to do about this. She can't leave her family. I wouldn't want her to anyway. I can't just up and leave. There is nothing I can fix. I just need to ride this out." Before Morgan has a chance to scold me further, Tina knocks and walks in carrying the most beautiful bouquet of flowers. I look point blank at Morgan. "You need to leave right now." She doesn't hesitate. She grabs a confused Tina and they leave. She knows I'm about to lose control. The door closes and I break down. I barely make it back into my chair before the sobs rack my body. Obviously, I don't need to look at the letter attached. I know they are from Kerry. I don't know how she did it, but she has delivered a piece of Ireland, a piece of her heart, to me here. I reach out and touch a forget-me-not stalk, gently rubbing the little blue flowers between my fingertips. My name is written in her handwriting on the outside of the envelope. How is that even possible? I sniffle and reach for the tissues on my desk. I'm a mess and I know it. I take a deep breath and open her letter.

Grace,
I hope you are doing well. I wanted to thank you for all that you have done for me and my family. You have the biggest heart out of anyone I've ever known and I will never forget you or our wonderful time together. As much as I miss you and us, I know that this is for the best. My life is so embedded in Ireland and yours in Dallas. I understand completely and I just wanted you to know that you will always be special and forever in my heart.
Forget me not,
Kerry

I don't know how long I've been on the floor of my office. I don't even remember how I got down here in the first place. I'm still clutching Kerry's letter. I've read it a thousand times already and my heart hurts every single time. I'm done. I ignore my intercom and manage to hit the do not disturb button on the phone on my way to the couch. Morgan knocks on my door, but I ignore her and the text messages she sends me. She speaks to me through the slit in the double doors and tells me it's after five and she's still at work. I half sniffle and half smile at that declaration. She hates working late.

"Call me tonight. If you don't, I'm going to hunt you down to make sure you're all right. Remember, I have keys to your office and your condo and I'm not afraid to use them." She waits for something from me.

I call out, "Thanks. I'll text you later." She gives me two knocks and leaves. That is code for see ya so I know she's okay with leaving me. I need to thank Kerry for sending me the flowers. I want to call her, but it's late there so I decide to send a text instead. It takes me about five minutes to compose something worth sending.

Thank you so much for the beautiful flowers. I have a little bit of Ireland here with me now. Your letter was incredibly kind and, of course, made me cry. I miss you.

I really don't want her to hurt as much as I hurt, so I try to keep my message simple, but let her know she's always on my mind. I'm surprised when she answers me back right away. I can tell she's typing me a message so I'm very still and watch my phone, afraid to breathe.

I meant every word. I miss you, too. And I showed the shop to someone today. He seems interested in it. I will contact him in the morning.

I don't even care about that right now. How are you? I find that I really don't care whether the flower shop sells or not. I just need her.

I'm okay. I've been better. Her message is unbelievably sad and uplifting at the same time. At least I know she is just as affected by the decision as I am.

Can I call you? I hold my breath as I wait for her answer.

Yes.

For a brief moment, I consider FaceTiming with her, but I'm a mess and blotchy from crying. Hearing her voice is a great first step.

"Hi, Grace," she says. My stomach twists and turns and I hold it to settle down. I will never get tired of hearing her saying my name.

"Hi." I don't know where to start. I want to tell her how much I miss her and this is the hardest thing I've ever had to do in my life and I cry all of the time now. I settle with something less dramatic. "The flowers are absolutely beautiful. Do I even want to know how you got them to me?"

"I called in a favor," she says. I can hear her smile at me even though we are thousands of miles apart.

"Surely, you have called in all of your favors by now."

"You would be surprised if you knew how many favors I've amassed over the time I've been selling houses," she says.

"And yet you continue to use them on me. It was a wonderful and very thoughtful surprise. Thank you so much." I'm so nervous right now. I'm afraid if I take a deep breath or if there's a lull, she will disappear.

"I just hated how fast things wrapped up. I'm completely unsettled," she says. My heart jumps at attention, waiting for her to elaborate. "But I know that this is the right thing to do." And then it sinks again.

"I know, but it still hurts." I need to change the subject or else I'll start crying again. "How's Ian? Were the clothes and toys a big hit?"

"Completely. Emma was beside herself. I haven't seen him in anything but what we bought for him. Now with the weather warming up a bit, he's able to wear the little short sleeved onesies. He's still too small for the toys, but I haven't given up," she says.

"If you need anything else for him, please let me know, okay?" I don't know what else I can say without making us both feel bad. "Tell me about the person who looked at the shop."

She slips into her professional voice. "Well, he's not a flower guy, unfortunately, but he's not big business either. He's looking to open up a bicycle repair shop and sell bikes. With so much bike traffic, it's not a bad idea."

"If he agrees to everything, how long does it take to close on a business?" I ask.

"It will take at least a month. That will give Leigh and Conor time to close everything up," she says.

I interrupt her. "How are they doing without Emma? Is Leigh working too hard?"

"I honestly don't know. I do know that with Conor out of school, he's able to hang out at the shop more though so I'm sure Leigh has him doing other things besides delivering flowers. He's a smart kid," she says.

"He's wonderful. Charming actually," I say, remembering our first meeting. "I miss everybody."

"They all still talk about you. Even Colleen asked about you. I saw her today when I took the client to lunch at her place."

"That's sweet. I miss everybody, too." Especially you, I silently add.

"Look, it's getting late and I know you need to get home and I need to get to bed. I'm glad you called me and I'm happy you like the flowers. Our time together was fantastic, Grace. Truly. I don't know what else I can say right now so I'm going to go." I want to tell her to stop. I want her to tell me she loves me and can't live without me. Why would she send me flowers if she wants this relationship to end?

"Kerry, wait. Is there anything I can do to change your mind? Obviously you are thinking about me, about us, because you sent me flowers. How am I not supposed to read into that?" I'm hanging on by a thread here.

"I thought about what I did, cutting us off that quickly, and it wasn't fair to either of us. Yes, it was the right thing to do, but I didn't want you to think that I'm heartless. I really want you to know that I had a wonderful time with you," she says.

"So, things are still going to be the same? The flowers change nothing? We are still going to move on, separately. Is that what you want?" I ask.

I hear her sigh. "I don't see an alternative. It's better to walk away now than later when we are both emotionally invested." I almost laugh at that. I'm beyond emotionally invested. I need to be my better self right now and agree.

"I know, I know. I just wanted to make sure," I say. We are both quiet for a few moments, neither of us knowing what to say. "Okay, go to sleep. I'm going to go home. Please just keep me posted on Bike Man."

I hear her smile. "I will."

"And thank you again for the flowers. Bye, Kerry," I say. I want to yell that I could never forget her or our time together. Instead, I quietly wait for her to say good-bye.

"Good-bye, Grace." The sadness in her voice breaks my heart. Again. I hang up and sit there for I don't know how long holding my phone staring off into space. What am I doing? What am I really doing with my life? I'm not invested in anything important here. Dallas is where I live and work. I have no roots other than a family I have nothing in common with, and who won't care if I leave. Kerry's everything is in Ireland. It's her home. It's where her heart is. It's who she is and I love her for it. Why am I still here? Why am I not chasing after the woman I love?

CHAPTER TWENTY-FOUR

"We will be on the ground in about twenty-five minutes," the pilot says. He should have just said "this will be the longest descent and twenty-five minutes really means twenty-five years" because this has been the longest flight of my life. Thankfully, I have an empty seat next to me because I really don't want to talk to anybody. The last two weeks were truly life changing. Literally. I hung up with Kerry that night and drove straight to Sherry's house. She begged me not to quit, told me we could work something out on a consultant basis. I still resigned from my position, but agreed to consult on future projects. I left Sherry's house and drove to Morgan's house. She saw the look on my face and knew right away.

"When do you leave?" I fucking love her. She didn't try to stop me. Instead, she offered to help me pack. That night. So adorably Morgan. We waited until the weekend and I gave her anything she wanted from my place. The rest of the belongings I boxed up and shipped over to Ireland in a container that still has two weeks to get to The Irish Garden. I couldn't get rid of my living room set and low profile bed. As much as I love Aunt Nola's furniture, I really love the luxury of my own stuff. I'll worry about where to put everything once it arrives. I brought two giant suitcases full of clothes and daily necessities on the plane with me.

Work did not take the news well. All of the departments were in complete shock. Sherry assured them that I'm willing to work as a consultant off-site and will remain in contact with them during the transition to another Creative Director. I recommended Alisa, but Sherry wants somebody with more experience. Morgan already nixed it. She doesn't want a complicated life. Everybody is afraid that they will have to work the same hours I did. I would've given more time, but two weeks is standard and honestly, Shumer & Bristol would have taken full advantage of me if I gave them more time. I worked with Brandon on getting my retirement transferred and other legal matters. Morgan is handling the sale of my condo with her real estate friend who assures me it will sell quickly, and I sold my SUV over the weekend. I'm completely walking away from my life to start a new one. I have no regrets. Yes, I will miss Morgan, but she promises to visit when work settles down.

We finally land and, of course, I have to wait forever to get my bags and head through customs. I feel like I'm the last one to reach the taxi line. Thankfully, the line is short and my wait is about ten minutes.

"The Irish Garden in Howth," I say. This cabbie grumbles, too, but he loads me up and we head out. I turn on my phone and see that I have missed a few calls from The Mulligan Group and two texts from Kerry.

You have an offer on the place. Full price! Please call me as soon as you can so I can extend your acceptance and we can get moving. Yay.

Grace, where are you? I don't want you to lose out on this deal. Should I accept?

It's after hours, so I know she's not at work anymore so I text her back.

Sorry. I'll call you in a bit. Don't do anything yet. I'm going to try to find her, but I need to unload my bags first. Naturally, the traffic is bad so I take a deep breath and sit back in the seat.

Watching the driver is only giving me motion sickness and pissing me off. I can't decide if he's driving like a little old lady on purpose for a bigger fare, or if he truly can't see the traffic around him. I tighten my seat belt. Like I want to die before I see Kerry. Then our story would become a folklore. As good as she is at telling tales, I really don't want to be the subject of one. By total chance, or intervention of a higher being, I see Leigh still at the shop. She's locking up as we are pulling up.

"Grace, you're here! Why are you here?" she asks. I can't help but hug her.

"I'm here for good, Leigh. The shop isn't closing," I tell her. She freaks me out by crying. Immediately. Not a gentle, work her way into it, but a break down sob. "Stop crying. Why are you crying?"

"I'm just so happy," she says. I give her another hug and she holds me until the cab driver clears his throat. I quickly pay him after he unloads my hefty suitcases and turn my attention back to Leigh. She unlocks the door for me and gives me her key. "Until we can get you your own set. It's too bad you just missed Kerry. She has a spare set."

"Where did she go?" I ask, knowing full well my voice sounds desperate. Leigh smiles at me.

"I don't know. She took off on her motorcycle about thirty minutes ago and said something about wanting to have a moment alone. She told us there was an offer on the place and she was just waiting to hear back from you," she says. I know exactly where she went.

"Grace, you're back." Conor pulls up beside me on his scooter with the biggest smile on his face.

"What happened to the van?" I ask.

"It's in the shop for an oil change and few other minor things. I'll pick it up in the morning."

I sigh and, with a rush of pure adrenaline, I reach over and place my hands on the handlebars. "Conor, I need your bike," I blurt out.

"Do you want me to give you a ride instead? I know you aren't crazy about driving here."

I don't want to give Kerry's secret spot away so I shake my head.

He shrugs and runs through instructions on how to work it, telling me tricks to get it started if it gets stubborn. I haven't driven a scooter in fifteen years. And this one is older than that. He hands me the helmet and wishes me well. "Be careful. I'm so happy for all of us." He's so genuine, I lean over and kiss him on his cheek. "I'll see you tomorrow. Bright and early. Thank you, Grace, for not shutting us down," he says. I jump on the scooter knowing that I'm about to face two of my biggest fears: driving in Ireland, and getting rejected by the woman I love.

"Wish me luck." I put Conor's massive helmet on. He laughs and takes a pic of me with his cell.

"If that shows up anywhere on social media, I'll have you sweeping the floors every day and taking out the trash." I point threateningly.

"I already do that now," he says. I give him an eye roll and gingerly ease into traffic. This drive will age me. It takes me a few minutes to get the feel of his scooter. Thankfully, the traffic is light and nobody rides my ass. They all give me space and pass when they can. I concentrate as hard as I can to drive on the left instead of the right. As long as I focus on the car in front of me, I stay in the correct lane. I start to panic a little because I'm not confident on where the dirt road is and it's starting to get dark out. I know the road is coming up soon because I start recognizing the view. I slow down and a few cars honk at me, but I don't care. My heart jumps when I see the familiar windy road and signal to turn. If she's not here, I'm going to cry and camp out until morning because I'm not driving this hunk of junk at night.

It seems like I follow the trail forever. I know I'm close because I recognize the stone wall on my left and the really cool tree with limbs that brush the ground. I see her bike up ahead. Apparently she hasn't heard the rinky-dink scooter. I know she's here though, and I feel hot and cold at the same time. I shake because I'm emotional and the fate of my life is going to be determined in just a few minutes. She's either going to be happy to see me, or I just made the biggest mistake of my life. I know Conor's scooter isn't designed for bumpy terrain so I park it and walk to the cliff. I have to stop myself from running to her. I touch her bike as I pass it, remembering the incredible time we had that one Sunday not too long ago. She is sitting on the grass, her knees up, her ankles crossed. Her hair is pulled back and she is completely lost in thought. I pluck a forget-me-not and walk softly over to her. I'm not sure what to do or say, but I just need to be with her right now. She still doesn't hear me. I'm right behind her. I put the flower in front of her and she jumps, completely startled. My heart breaks at the tears she's clearly been crying for so long. I kneel beside her and she falls into my arms. I don't know when I start crying, but we are both sobbing and clinging to each other.

"Grace, what are you doing here?" She pushes me away only to stare at me in disbelief. "What are you doing here?"

"I can't be away from you. You're everything I've ever wanted in this lifetime. You are smart, sexy, fun, passionate, stubborn, and I'm unbelievably head-over-heels in love with you. I love your hopes, and your dreams, and your passion for life. I love your family, and how close you are with them. I miss you. I need you. I'm here, Kerry. I'm here in Ireland for good." So much for feeling her emotions out first before I open up. She stares at me, her eyes searching mine, and I'm about ready to pass out from embarrassment. "And I really miss Abram. I can't imagine my life without him either." For some reason, that breaks her. She sobs again and I don't know if it's because she's happy or completely sad. Horrible thoughts are in my head right now. Maybe she met somebody. Maybe she always had somebody. No, maybe she got married! My heart is pounding. Every beat feels like five minutes apart, when I know it's really beating unbelievably fast in my chest. "Please, Kerry, please say something. I'm dying here." She cries even harder. "At least let me know if you want me here."

"Yes! Oh my God, Grace. I just can't believe you're here. How? What? Why?" She touches my face, my hair, my shoulders. She's crying and hiccupping with laughter, which is surprisingly confusing.

"I hate my life without you in it. I have nothing in Dallas. I rarely talk to my dad or my brother so they aren't going to miss me. I'll probably do consulting work for Shumer & Bristol so that will keep me busy when The Irish Garden is slow. I sold my car, I put my condo on the market, and my stuff should be here in two weeks. I'm going to live above the flower shop and I'm going to date you and do everything right. You are what I want. You." I kiss her softly.

She pulls me close to her again. "Grace, I'm just so happy. I love you so much. I've been dead inside since Dallas. I didn't want to tell you because I didn't think it was fair to put that pressure on you." She cries harder.

"Are you kidding me? I was so worried you wouldn't be happy that I'm here. I thought maybe you found someone else. You sounded so final the last time we spoke."

She puts her forehead against mine. "That was the hardest thing I've ever had to do. Let you go. My heart hurt and every breath I took was painful. I've been a mess for weeks." She kisses me softly at first, then possessively. I submit willingly. "Sit down with me. Our first of every sunset in Ireland." She sits down, but instead of sitting next to her, I straddle her lap. "What are you doing, love?" I want to hear her call me that every day of my life. Love.

"I want to look at you right now. Aunt Nola waited a long time before she confessed her love to Kate and I don't want to waste any time with you. She wouldn't want me to either. See? I'm learning so much from her." I lock my fingers behind her neck.

"You are missing out on a great sunset." She pretends to look around me.

"I'm not missing out on anything. I have the one thing I want right in front of me." I'm rewarded with another passionate kiss.

"It's a beautiful sunset," she teases. Her eyes haven't left mine.

I sigh playfully and twist around to see it. "You're right. It's beautiful. There. Are you happy now?"

"I couldn't be happier." We kiss and as we heat up, Kerry unbuttons my shirt after pulling it from my jeans. I moan at the familiarity of her touch. I've missed her so much and I promise right then and there that I will do everything in my power to keep her happy for the rest of our lives. "How about we head back to Howth and celebrate the fact that you're here? And speaking of which, how did you get here?" I point to Conor's scooter off in the distance. She throws her head back and laughs. "Wait. You drove in Ireland?"

I shrug like it's no big deal even though I'm still shaky about it. "The things I will do for love." She hugs me tightly until I squeal with happiness and alarm as my oxygen is cut off.

"I love you, Grace Danner. Let's go celebrate."

"I love you, too, Kerry Mulligan. I will go back to Howth with you and celebrate, but only under one condition."

"Whatever you want, love."

"You drive."

Epilogue

Six Months Later

"Are you sure we're ready to have Christmas here?" I'm completely stressed out about twenty people and tiny Ian here at our place. We're still new hands at this farming thing, especially me, and trying to organize a major family dinner may have been a bit premature.

"Love, we are only responsible for the turkey. Everybody else is bringing a side. Please don't worry. I'm sure it will be wonderful." Kerry leans over and kisses me, trying to ease my nerves. "Our place looks great. You've done a remarkable job here. And all of the stubborn animals are staying in their pens for a change. Today is going to be perfect."

Yesterday was a hot mess. I came home after closing up The Irish Garden for the holiday to several of our goats standing on the front wall by the road. And to top that off, Kerry didn't latch the sunroom when she left and two goats made their way into it, eating the few plants I managed not to kill over the fall, as well as a few cushions on the wicker furniture. I was livid. The goats didn't care. Kerry just laughed and told me this will happen. I grabbed Abram and hid in the bedroom until Kerry came upstairs to tell me everything was cleaned up. I apologized for being upset by it, and she apologized that it happened in the first place.

She also assured me that this wasn't going to be the one and only time it would happen.

"Do you think you will be able to take a nap today?" Kerry asks. We've been up since four this morning.

"I doubt it. I still need to get presentable and our guests will be here in three hours." Conor, who now lives in the apartment above The Irish Garden, is getting back from his family's celebration and will be here tonight, as will Leigh and Charles. They are, after all, my family, too.

"Thank you for doing this." Kerry takes me in her arms, giving me a much needed and appreciated break. "I love you."

"I love you, too. You are my favorite Christmas present. Ever," I say.

"Thank you for giving up everything to be with me. I'm the luckiest girl in the whole world. Do you want my present now or after everybody leaves?" Usually after opening presents we end up having really great sex and since we are pressed for time, I tell her we should wait until everybody leaves. Besides, I want it to just be us when I propose.

About the Author

Kris Bryant grew up a military brat living in several different countries before her family settled down in the Midwest when she was twelve. Books were her only form of entertainment overseas, and she read anything and everything within her reach. Reading eventually turned into writing when she decided she didn't like the way some of the novels ended and wanted to give the characters she fell in love with the ending she thought they so deserved.

Earning a B.A. in English from the University of Missouri, Kris focused more on poetry, and after some encouragement from her girlfriend, decided to tackle her own book.

Kris can be contacted at krisbryantbooks@gmail.com

Website: http://www.krisbryant.net

Books Available from Bold Strokes Books

Escape in Time by Robyn Nyx. Working in the past is hell on your future. (978-1-62639-855-9)

Forget-Me-Not by Kris Bryant. Is love worth walking away from the only life you've ever dreamed of? (978-1-62639-865-8)

Highland Fling by Anna Larner. On vacation in the Scottish Highlands, Eve Eddison falls for the enigmatic forestry officer Moira Burns, despite Eve's best friend's campaign to convince her that Moira will break her heart. (978-1-62639-853-5)

Phoenix Rising by Rebecca Harwell. As Storm's Quarry faces invasion from a powerful neighbor, a mysterious newcomer with powers equal to Nadya's challenges everything she believes about herself and her future (978-1-62639-913-6)

Soul Survivor by I. Beacham. Sam and Joey have given up on hope, but when fate brings them together it gives them a chance to change each other's life and make dreams come true. (978-1-62639-882-5)

Strawberry Summer by Melissa Brayden. When Margaret Beringer's first love Courtney Carrington returns to their small town, she must grapple with their troubled past and fight the temptation for a very delicious future. (978-1-62639-867-2)

The Girl on the Edge of Summer by J.M. Redmann. Micky Knight accepts two cases, but neither is the easy investigation it appears. The past is never past—and young girls lead complicated, even dangerous lives. (978-1-62639-687-6)

Unknown Horizons by CJ Birch. The moment Lieutenant Alison Ash steps aboard the Persephone, she knows her life will never be the same. (978-1-62639-938-9)

Divided Nation, United Hearts by Yolanda Wallace. In a nation torn in two by a most uncivil war, can love conquer the divide? (978-1-62639-847-4)

Fury's Bridge by Brey Willows. What if your life depended on someone who didn't believe in your existence? (978-1-62639-841-2)

Lightning Strikes by Cass Sellars. When Parker Duncan and Sydney Hyatt's one-night stand turns to more, both women must fight demons past and present to cling to the relationship neither of them thought she wanted. (978-1-62639-956-3)

Love in Disaster by Charlotte Greene. A professor and a celebrity chef are drawn together by chance, but can their attraction survive a natural disaster? (978-1-62639-885-6)

Secret Hearts by Radclyffe. Can two women from different worlds find common ground while fighting their secret desires? (978-1-62639-932-7)

Sins of Our Fathers by A. Rose Mathieu. Solving gruesome murder cases is only one of Elizabeth Campbell's challenges; another is her growing attraction to the female detective who is hell-bent on keeping her client in prison. (978-1-62639-873-3)

The Sniper's Kiss by Justine Saracen. The power of a kiss: it can swell your heart with splendor, declare abject submission, and sometimes blow your brains out. (978-1-62639-839-9)

Troop 18 by Jessica L. Webb. Charged with uncovering the destructive secret that a troop of RCMP cadets has been hiding, Andy must put aside her worries about Kate and uncover the conspiracy before it's too late. (978-1-62639-934-1)

Worthy of Trust and Confidence by Kara A. McLeod. FBI Special Agent Ryan O'Connor is about to discover the hard way that when you can only handle one type of answer to a question, it really is better not to ask. (978-1-62639-889-4)

Amounting to Nothing by Karis Walsh. When mounted police officer Billie Mitchell steps in to save beautiful murder witness Merissa Karr, worlds collide on the rough city streets of Tacoma, Washington. (978-1-62639-728-6)

Becoming You by Michelle Grubb. Airlie Porter has a secret. A deep, dark, destructive secret that threatens to engulf her if she can't find the courage to face who she really is and who she really wants to be with. (978-1-62639-811-5)

Birthright by Missouri Vaun. When spies bring news that a swordswoman imprisoned in a neighboring kingdom bears the Royal mark, Princess Kathryn sets out to rescue Aiden, true heir to the Belstaff throne. (978-1-62639-485-8)

Crescent City Confidential by Aurora Rey. When romance and danger are in the air, writer Sam Torres learns the Big Easy is anything but. (978-1-62639-764-4)

Love Down Under by MJ Williamz. Wylie loves Amarina, but if Amarina isn't out, can their relationship last? (978-1-62639-726-2)

Privacy Glass by Missouri Vaun. Things heat up when Nash Wiley commandeers a limo and her best friend for a late drive out to the beach: Champagne on ice, seat belts optional, and privacy glass a must. (978-1-62639-705-7)

The Impasse by Franci McMahon. A horse packing excursion into the Montana Wilderness becomes an adventure of terrifying proportions for Miles and ten women on an outfitter led trip. (978-1-62639-781-1)

The Right Kind of Wrong by PJ Trebelhorn. Bartender Quinn Burke is happy with her life as a playgirl until she realizes she can't fight her feelings any longer for her best friend, bookstore owner Grace Everett. (978-1-62639-771-2)

Wishing on a Dream by Julie Cannon. Can two women change everything for the chance at love? (978-1-62639-762-0)

A Quiet Death by Cari Hunter. When the body of a young Pakistani girl is found out on the moors, the investigation leaves Detective Sanne Jensen facing an ordeal she may not survive. (978-1-62639-815-3)

Buried Heart by Laydin Michaels. When Drew Chambliss meets Cicely Jones, her buried past finds its way to the surface—will they survive its discovery or will their chance at love turn to dust? (978-1-62639-801-6)

Escape: Exodus Book Three by Gun Brooke. Aboard the Exodus ship *Pathfinder*, President Thea Tylio still holds Caya Lindemay, a clairvoyant changer, in protective custody, which has devastating consequences endangering their relationship and the entire Exodus mission. (978-1-62639-635-7)

Genuine Gold by Ann Aptaker. New York, 1952. Outlaw Cantor Gold is thrown back into her honky-tonk Coney Island past, where crime and passion simmer in a neon glare. (978-1-62639-730-9)

Into Thin Air by Jeannie Levig. When her girlfriend disappears, Hannah Lewis discovers her world isn't as orderly as she thought it was. (978-1-62639-722-4)

Night Voice by CF Frizzell. When talk show host Sable finally acknowledges her risqué radio relationship with a mysterious caller, she welcomes a *real* relationship with local tradeswoman Riley Burke. (978-1-62639-813-9)

Raging at the Stars by Lesley Davis. When the unbelievable theories start revealing themselves as truths, can you trust in the ones who have conspired against you from the start? (978-1-62639-720-0)

She Wolf by Sheri Lewis Wohl. When the hunter becomes the hunted, more than love might be lost. (978-1-62639-741-5)

Smothered and Covered by Missouri Vaun. The last person Nash Wiley expects to bump into over a two a.m. breakfast at Waffle House is her college crush, decked out in a curve-hugging law enforcement uniform. (978-1-62639-704-0)

The Butterfly Whisperer by Lisa Moreau. Reunited after ten years, can Jordan and Sophie heal the past and rediscover love or will differing desires keep them apart? (978-1-62639-791-0)

The Devil's Due by Ali Vali. Cain and Emma Casey are awaiting the birth of their third child, but as always in Cain's world, there are new and old enemies to face in post Katrina-ravaged New Orleans. (978-1-62639-591-6)

Widows of the Sun-Moon by Barbara Ann Wright. With immortality now out of their grasp, the gods of Calamity fight amongst themselves, egged on by the mad goddess they thought they'd left behind. (978-1-62639-777-4)